Ecochondriacs

Ecochondriacs

THE NO QUARTER NOVEMBER NOVEL

Douglas Wilson

canonpress

MOSCOW, IDAHO

Published by Canon Press
P.O. Box 8729, Moscow, ID 83843
800.488.2034 | www.canonpress.com

Cover design by James Engerbretson.
Interior formatting by Samuel Dickison.

Printed in the United States of America.

Library of Congress Cataloging-in-Publication Data

Wilson, Douglas, 1953- author.
Ecochondriacs : a no quarter November novel / Douglas Wilson.
Paperback edition. | Moscow, Idaho : Canon Press, 2021.
LCCN 2020051662 | ISBN 9781952410802 (paperback)
LCSH: Political fiction. | GSAFD: Suspense fiction.
Classification: LCC PS3623.I57875 E28 2021 | DDC 813/.6—dc23
LC record available at https://lccn.loc.gov/2020051662

20 21 22 23 24 25 26 27 28 29   10 9 8 7 6 5 4 3 2 1

This book is dedicated to Mark Steyn,
to whom I am indebted for various things,
including my introduction to the word *ecochondriacs*.

Contents

CHAPTER 1

Unexpected Guests

COUNTDOWN

Dr. Helen Greene let herself into her brown Annapolis town-house apartment, kicked off her shoes by the front door, set the small bag of groceries down on the kitchen counter, and then went back to lock and bolt the front door. She lived in a nice neighborhood, but it was only three blocks away from one that wasn't so nice, and she had always been a careful sort.

She circled back into her living room, enjoying how the carpet felt on her sore feet. It had been the day of days, and was actually about to get a good deal day-er than that. This, in fact, was going to be the day-iest of all her born days. If you threw in the next morning, it was going to be epic.

As she walked by her home office laptop—which was lined up perfectly straight with the lip of the desk and perfectly

1

perpendicular with the two mechanical pencils on the right side of the computer (there was nothing else on her most *immaculate* desk)—her eye caught a notification from Steven Lee, her one-time advisor and mentor from grad school. Dr. Lee was now the current head of her research group, and up to this year she had thought that his "gruff" manners were the mark of great genius. But over the last several months, she had started to wonder if they were really an indicator of a soaring ego, as opposed to a soaring intellect. That thought had occurred to her a time or three.

Helen had been appointed to the research group last year—and it really was quite the honor for someone her age. The group was an international task force on climate change, and was the most prestigious of the lot—the lot consisting of all the other task forces, each one scrambling for money and throwing the occasional elbow. Fueled by massive amounts of money from multiple governments and international organizations, climate change research was a growth industry, a boom town, a cash cow that emitted no methane, only cash. So the fact that Lee's group was the most prestigious of the bunch was really saying something.

Usually no one was *ever* invited to join this group unless they were at least five years out of grad school and had made some kind of independent glory for themselves when it came to publication in the kinds of journals that exuded significantly higher levels of that special numinous and scientific glow. Although the source of that radiant gravitas was mysterious, you knew it when you saw it on a resume. And Helen had only been working at establishing her resume for three years, with the same number of significant publications, three thus far, and so the invitation had come to her as a genuine shock. Such an invitation had been her goal all along, and was precisely what she had been driving for, but she had assumed she was going to be in the salt mines of schlub research for at least two more years. But since that exuberant day, since her appointment, as she was a careful sort, she had been doing her level best to pull her own weight. Her labors had been, she *thought*, paying off. It was not the kind of place where anybody ever said "good job," but it was the kind of place where displeasure was cogently expressed without any stinting, and she had not been on the receiving end of any of *that*. So she thought she could say that she was doing well in her job.

She was quite an attractive woman, but she had some years before decided that she wasn't really all that attractive, and that if she were to make something of herself she needed to really give herself to her studies. She prided herself on her scholarship, and kept all her girl stuff in a back room somewhere. That decision, ironically, had been the result of some mean things another girl on her junior high cheerleading squad had said to her, and Helen had really no idea that the girl had said them because of how pretty Helen was.

At any rate, Helen sat down, clicked the email thread open, and according to her usual custom, scrolled down to the bottom of the initial email so that she could get the context. The subject line read "What's one more lie . . .?" which she thought a curious tag, but as the next few minutes passed, her curiosity gradually turned to horror and dismay as she scrolled up through the exchanges. They were between Steven Lee, her boss, and

Martin Chao, and Leonid Ravinsky, the triumvirate of Climate Change. World-respected authorities on the subject, and here they were all chortling at what a scam it all was. They didn't believe a lick of it.

Helen just sat there, gobsmacked on more than one level. The first had to do with her own worldview. They didn't believe *any* of it. She had believed *all* of it, heart and soul. No missionary had ever gone to deepest Africa with more devotion in her heart for the lost than Helen had gone off to grad school. Now she suddenly felt like an archbishop would have felt had he been goaded into opening up his cathedral's most precious reliquary to a team of scientists so that they could carbon date the finger bone of St. Andrew, only to have them come back to him with the hot news that the finger bone was only seven hundred years old, a time nowhere close to the time of St. Andrew, and that it was, moreover, the finger bone of a chimpanzee. It was the chimpanzee part that hurt.

The comparison may be inexact, but she felt *something* like that.

The second level had to do with her sense of personal betrayal and astonishment. These were men she had respected on a personal level, and here they were joking about all the money they were raking in, and making fun of all the rubes who gave it to them, and what a laugher the whole thing was. There was even a joke about how easy the women at the big climate change conferences were. Thank heaven *that* wasn't mixed up in her story with any of them. But she then thought, rather suddenly, that she *still* must be numbered among those gullible women in their eyes, and she could feel her cheeks getting hot.

But the third level of difficulty dawned on her a little more slowly. This last one was a stinker. She got to the last email at the top, in reply to the rest of the thread, the one that Steven Lee had sent directly to her. It said, without any fanfare, "Please delete the previous thread without reading it. It was sent to you by mistake, and does contain some confidential and proprietary information."

Without hesitating, and without thinking about it too carefully, she quickly typed, "No worries. Will not read," and clicked *send*.

Then she jumped up immediately and walked around her apartment three times. How should she conduct herself at the offices the next day? How was she going to *act*? What was she to do? She was needed there by ten a.m., and she had a report to present right after lunch, at one p.m. That part was all right because she was the sort of person who always completed reports a week before they were due. But how was she going to *act*?

Everything about her situation was a complete and total novelty to her. She had lost her surface-level evangelical faith in high school, and even the memory of it was greatly dimmed by her undergraduate days. By the time she had hit grad school, her atheism was in full flower, and so naturally she fit right in. But since the first appearance of that atheism, because she was the kind of woman who never did what's not done, she had never faced any kind of ethical dilemma. She had simply memorized the rules of her new chosen discipline, and followed them loyally. If there was a climate change line anywhere, she colored inside it.

And here she was now, with a full-blown ethical dilemma. This was an ethical dilemma with a fire in the attic. This was an ethical dilemma with the brakes gone clean out at the very top of the switchback grade. There was no God, and so no help there. The rules of her discipline—well, the ethics code for climatologists—as she knew full well, had been drafted by Dr. Steven Lee, and helpfully edited by his friends Martin and Leonid.

Should she confront them? Should she just lie and keep her head down? Should she laugh about it openly, in a worldly-wise way, and assure them that their secret was safe with her? Join with them in the shake-down? She felt like her skull was a bone box full of water and that somebody had dumped about twenty-five Alka-Seltzer tablets into it.

She put her groceries away, more than a little bit agitated. She noticed this when it dawned on her that she had put the milk into the fridge at least three times, and must therefore have taken it out at least two times. She shook her head violently, and forced herself back to the task. When she eventually got *that* job completed, and it ought to have been a simple task, she thought about dinner momentarily, and turned away from that idea with a shudder. No appetite at *all*.

Helen then decided to get up early in order to sit down at her desk with a clear head, and work it all out. She *had* to work it all out. Tomorrow was Monday morning. She had to go to work in the morning, so she would work it all out. She set her alarm for six a.m., took a hot shower and went to bed. Despite an hour or two of tossing and tossing and tossing—Helen did not toss and turn, but always went clockwise—she eventually fell into a fitful and uneasy sleep.

CHAPTER 2

Making Messes

LAUNCH

Despite her agitation, she did manage to fall asleep, albeit fitfully. And *that* lasted until about five a.m., when she sat bolt upright in bed, gasping for air. She was a woman who had an odd quirk in her thinking processes, shared only by a handful of others. During that strange gray time between waking and sleeping, she had the kind of mind that would solve problems for her, or remember things, or come up with great ideas. This characteristic had actually been her friend on many occasions. In fact, it was being her friend *now*, only it didn't feel like it. This time it just scared her sideways and silly.

Just last week, Steven Lee had been talking to somebody a bit too loudly in the alcove where the vending machines were, and she couldn't remember who he had been talking to. But she had been just around the corner at her desk, and he was talking about some software he had just installed that could tell you if a person had read the email you had sent them. Not only so, but you could tell if they had forwarded to anybody. They couldn't yet tell *who* you had forwarded it to, but they could tell you how many. She wasn't sure if it could tell if you transferred it to a thumb drive or anything like that. She wasn't even sure if something like that was possible. The one thing she was sure of was that she needed to scramble out of bed, which was exactly what she did.

She threw on some clothes and went over to stare at her computer. She needed to decide what to do. As in, right now. Should she act like nothing had happened and just brazen it out? But what if her mouth filled up with cotton balls, and she started to talk to her boss like the guiltiest person on the planet? What about that? Should she copy the email thread onto a thumb drive? What would she do with it then? She didn't want it. Who would she give it to? And could he tell with his software if she were to do that?

She just stood there wavering, like an aspen in a stiff breeze. Suddenly she sat down, not quite sure why, pulled a thumb drive out of drawer, and copied the whole thread over, and then threw the drive in her purse. "*That's* not a plan," she muttered to herself. It was the most courageous thing she had ever done in her life, but she was not aware of that in the moment. She was simply in a state.

And it is likely that she would be there still, rocking back and forth in her chair, had events not started taking on a life of their own. It was about five thirty in the morning by this point, and she suddenly froze, startled by a scraping noise on her back patio, like a lawn chair being kicked, which is exactly what it was. She stood up and grabbed her purse with the goods in it, darted back to her bedroom, and pulled a Glock out of the drawer by the head of her bed.

Her politics were of course left of center, and so she had often felt guilty about having a firearm, not to mention a tad inconsistent, but whenever that feeling came over her she just thought how bad the neighborhood was just three blocks over. She could live with the inconsistency, and there had been times when she thought she might not be alive without it.

She jumped back to the door of the bedroom, gun raised, just like she had seen in movies, and held her breath. In the dim morning light, she started to stare intently at the gun to make sure the safety was off. Then she remembered that Glocks don't have safeties, like the kind man at the store had explained a couple of times. After that, she didn't have to wait very long. The glass in her sliding glass door shattered, from top to bottom, and a man with a green ski mask stepped through it. Another man, in another ski mask, this one a dull red, stepped in right behind him. The second man was about six inches shorter.

"Well, miss," the first one said, "we've just come for those emails. There's a good girl."

And then the second one spoke, and a spark of hope flickered to life down in Helen's chest. These men didn't sound too bright. "Yeah, miss," the second one said. "We don't bite. We won't *hurt* you." And he said this in a fashion that convinced her with absolute certainty that if she cooperated with them in *any* way, she would be dead before breakfast. That caused a pang because she had skipped dinner last night and was pretty hungry. But she silently hissed at herself not to be silly, and tried to focus on the intruders.

Her living room and bedroom and office were all still gray in that early morning way that unlit houses have, but she could see the two men both clearly outlined against the first light of dawn coming in from the patio. She was pretty sure they would not able to see her as clearly. So she thought about it for just a second or so, lowered her gun, and coolly shot the first man in the leg. The second man yelped and jumped behind the couch. Helen ran across her bedroom and out the door on the other side of the bedroom, a door that emptied into the hallway that ran out to the front door.

And out the front door *she* ran, with no thought or plan or strategy or prayer. Her Glock was in her right hand, and the purse in her left. She was wearing sneakers, and sweat pants, and an old T-shirt from the Climate Change picnic of the year before, and her brown hair was tied back in an early morning pony tail. The street in front of her house was deserted in both directions, with one solitary and very welcome exception.

Sitting still in the middle of the road was a black Tahoe, the one that belonged to her neighbor across the street, one Cody Vance. Cody Vance was a nice man, and not at all like the two thugs. The car was stationary because Cody had heard the gunshot, and was trying to sort out where it could have come from, it having sounded much closer than three blocks away. As soon as she saw the car, the only possible plan she could adopt came into her mind, and so she dashed for the passenger side door. She didn't need to run as fast as she did because the second man was still behind the couch, starting to get up and ignoring the pleas of his friend, who was bleeding all over Helen's carpet. That carpet would have to be replaced.

Helen pulled at the handle a couple of times, missed both times in her excitement, and then finally got the door open, and jumped in. "Go," she said. "*Please,*" she added, remembering her manners.

Cody stepped on it, and pulled briskly away. "I suppose," he said, as he accelerated, "that this is the kind of situation that will be explained after a few blocks?"

"Yes," Helen said, somewhat breathlessly.

"And will the explanation include the fact that you have a gun in your hand?"

"Yes," she said again.

But before anything more could be said, and before they got to the corner, Cody's back window shattered as a bullet went through it. "Yikes!" he said, and Helen screamed a little stifled scream. The second man had finally run out the front door, managed to get off one shot, and then he jumped into the car that he and his friend had driven there. He promptly peeled out after the Tahoe, leaving the first man still on Helen's carpet, soon to be discovered by some inquisitive policemen who were summoned by various neighbors on account of the two gunshots, and who found it curious that the front door of Helen's townhouse was wide open. When they came inside, they were full of questions for Maurice, lying there as he was on the carpet, and unable, because of both time and pain, to come up with a good story for why he was there in that condition. But I am getting ahead.

Cody took a hard right, and stomped on the accelerator. "Whatever you do," he said, "don't put that gun away."

He looked in the rear view mirror at just the moment when the second man—his name was Leon, since we are now needing to keep track of everybody—took the corner on two wheels. There was a long slow curve ahead, which Cody accelerated into, his mind trying accelerate at the same time. Helen kept turning around to look out the shattered back window, and in the midst of one swivel noticed that Cody's eyes were glittering with excitement. He was *enjoying* this. He downshifted, and Helen rocked in the seat.

There was a short cut to work that Cody usually took, about a quarter of mile away, and he was trying to think about it clearly with his brain full of adrenaline. His question was whether or not that short cut would be visible from the road he was currently on. If the gunman kept on this road, like Cody wanted, what would he be able to *see*? He decided to take the gamble when the time came, took a hard right onto a frontage road, roared another thirty yards, and then another hard right onto his tricksy short cut route, hidden back in the trees. And as the Tahoe disappeared down that country lane, his eye was fixed on his rear view mirror, and he saw Leon's green car flash by on the road he had just left. That car showed no signs of second thoughts, or of slowing down in any way. Leon was a not very bright man, and was intent on his mission in what was now entirely the wrong direction. Cody sped up again. They were safe for the moment.

He drove a mile or so, and then pulled into the parking lot of an abandoned cement factory. "Okay," he said. "We are safe for the present. *What* is going on?"

Helen had been thinking frantically about what on earth she was going to say when this inevitable moment came, and she hadn't come up with anything much.

"Um," she said. "They were trying to kill me."

"So I gathered," he said. "Were there any reasons associated with this? Did you have dirt on Hillary or something?"

Helen sat up a little straighter in her seat. *That* was the kind of joke that used to offend her every single Thanksgiving. Her extended family hailed from places like Oklahoma and Alabama, and there wasn't an Arkancide joke in existence that hadn't been told in her presence at least three times. A little starch started to creep into her demeanor, until she suddenly remembered that Steven Lee, the man who had apparently put out this hit on her, was actually a friend of Hillary's. Or a big donor anyway.

"Um," she said again, "I am not quite sure."

"Okay," he said. "Any reasonable guesses?"

"I am really not sure I should say anything."

"Okay," he said again. "There is nothing for it then but for me to take you back to your place. The cops will no doubt be there by now. You will probably feel better talking to them about it anyway."

"No!" She almost shouted. "I mean, please no," she said more quietly. She knew how well-connected Steven Lee and his crowd were, on a global level, and she knew that steering or managing a local police department would be a morsel of baked goods for them, otherwise known to the general populace as a piece of cake.

"Now look," Cody said. "I am more than happy to drive you away from a life-threatening situation for a mile or two. But any more than that and the price of your ticket is that you tell me your best guess for what's going on. If I find your story credible, then I will take you somewhere safe, if we are able to figure out where that might be. If not, we go back to your place."

"All right," she said, submissively. "I don't want to tell you the content of the emails, at least not right now, but some compromising emails were sent to me by accident. Compromising to the senders, I mean. I read them, also by accident, and then got a message from my boss telling me to delete them. But I had already read them, and he has a software program that tells him when somebody has opened and read the email he sent. I just remembered *that* this morning, just before those two goons showed up."

"*Two* goons?" Cody said.

"I shot one before you rescued me."

Cody turned in his seat and looked at her hard. "You *shot* one?"

"Well, in the leg."

He sat quietly. "My name is Cody," he eventually said.

"Yes, I know," she said. "I met you at the neighborhood block party last summer. My name is Helen, in case you forgot."

"I do remember meeting you," he said. "But I am terrible with names. Many apologies."

Another few moments went by, as did a few cars on the road by the old cement factory.

"So what do you do? CIA? Interpol? It must be exciting work that could result in your boss putting out a contract on you."

"I teach a climatology course at Yale. And I do climatology research at the Smithsonian."

"What was in that email? Why partly cloudy always means rain?"

She glared at him. "Climate, not weather."

"Right," he said. "I keep forgetting these important distinctions."

"And what do you do?"

"I teach New Testament studies for Liberty University online. And I live up here in Annapolis because I have a research fellowship on the history of second century manuscripts of the gospels, mostly all in fragments."

"Oh," she said, hoping that no disapproval had come through in her voice. But it had.

She sat for a moment, shaking her head. Eventually, she just said it. "Well, I suppose I had better tell you . . . Not that I want to. But I do need to."

THE DYING CANDIDATE

Brock Tilton stared at his personal physician balefully. He trusted his doctor's medical expertise completely, but did not trust the "life coach" lessons that Timothy Zizouzias would try to offer him from time to time. Zizouzias was the one who had, about six months earlier, delivered the news to him about his congenital heart disease, and how serious it really was. He was also the same doctor whose complete silence had been purchased for quite a handsome fee. When it came to raw physical stamina, Tilton was something of a draft horse, and that is why deception on the point was even a possibility. He didn't *look* like he was going to keel over any minute but, Zizouzias assured him, that was coming up pretty soon. "Fitness is not the same thing as health," the doctor had just said. "You can just be stubborn for a little bit, and maybe a little bit more. But that's it."

The thing that made this interesting on a broader scale was that Tilton was the Democratic nominee for the presidency, and on some days his race against Bryan McFetridge looked like it was neck-and-neck, and other days it looked as though he had a better than even chance. Other days McFetridge was ahead. This was according to their internal polls, as opposed to the public jokes that were good for nothing other than trying to manipulate the public. Anybody who believed the polls offered up for public consumption was as big a joke as the polls were.

Anything could happen, as Tilton well knew, and so he was resolved that one of the things that was *not* going to happen was any news getting out that the Democratic nominee had only months to live, six or eight, give or take. And as it happened, Tilton's veep nomination was a young up-and-comer named Del Martin, barely old enough to be president.

Depending on how stressful the campaign appeared to be to observers and bystanders, Zizouzias would come in periodically with life lessons from an aspiring life coach. If only Brock retired, took it easy, hired the very best physicians—he had lots of money—he could probably live another couple of years. And if he got a good match for a heart transplant, he could go fishing for even longer.

The problem with all such proposals was that even though Brock Tilton was a cold-hearted bastard, he did have one hot passion. That one hot passion was the jet fuel he used in order to fly his insane ambition up to his own private heights. By this point in his career, he almost qualified as an astronaut.

If he could just be elected to the presidency, and have *that* particular accomplishment next to his name, he didn't care what happened after that. If he lost the election, he wouldn't mind having a battery of doctors take a look at his ticker, but *that* would likely mean kissing good-bye to any chance of running for the presidency in the future. And he did not want to take that chance. He would rather be president for three months and then dead than not be president for three years and then dead. He had worked it all out in his head, and it hadn't taken that long. He was a man who knew what he wanted.

Nobody knew about this particular medical issue except for Timothy Zizouzias. Nobody. The party didn't know, his advisors didn't know, his donors didn't know, his wife didn't know, the God Brock didn't believe in didn't know, and his running mate Del Martin didn't know. The only two who knew about it were sitting in that little doctor's room, staring coldly at each other. It was not cold most of the time, for they had an understanding, but it was cold sometimes, like now.

"I know you don't want to hear about leaving the race," Zizouzias said. "I just have to bring it up from time to time in order to salve what's left of my medical conscience."

"The only salve you need is cash," Tilton said, "and I have made sure you will have plenty of that. More than you will know what to do with, more than was decent, and way more than market rate. If we were to judge the state of your conscience by how much cash it took to make it feel better, we might have to conclude that your conscience doesn't have a lot to say to us in this conversation."

Zizouzias winced and decided to drop it. "Are you going to tell Del Martin?"

Tilton shook his head brusquely. "No need. He's a big boy. A bit too pragmatic for my taste, but he will be much better than that cardboard cutout McFetridge. And if the base turns out in sufficient numbers to get me in, they will remain powerful enough to keep Del from getting seduced by all those Wall Street boys. Man, I *hate* those guys."

He was talking this way because Tilton was a hard leftist from the old school. He had been a red-diaper baby, and was steeped in the wit and wisdom of Saul Alinsky from his earliest days. But over the years he had learned the delicate art of covering over his communism with the Verathane of a populist and democratic feel-good jargon. As a consequence, his whole career was pretty shiny by this point, not to mention sticky. However, all close political observers knew that Tilton was the closest thing to an actual Trotskyite ever to have an actual chance of living in the White House.

The fact that he was virtually a communist was well known in right-wing circles, but the mainstream media was resolved to see nothing whatever that was problematic to the left. And there wasn't much room to their left anyhow. He could count on them to prevent the word from getting around widely. He could also count on them not to circulate the photos of him partying with Fidel Castro. He could count on them for lots of things. Somebody could prove that he had been Vladimir Lenin's roommate in college, and it wouldn't make a bit of difference. He wouldn't even need to point out that the chronologies didn't fit at all—Lenin having died long before Tilton was even born. There was that, and it would be a cinch to prove, but it wouldn't even be necessary. He could grant the facts behind the devastating "roommate ad" that the RNC just put out, and that would not change his levels of support from the media.

Tilton stopped his daydream and shook his head again. "No. No, Martin will be fine. He will wake up one day, not knowing that he is going to become president that day. He will be fine if the base yells at him loud enough, and frequently enough. And I think they are in the mood to do just that."

Their conversation then turned back to practical medical matters, and the regimen of medications that Zizouzias was using to keep Tilton vertical and somewhat energetic. It was a complicated regimen of pills, and somewhat experimental, but Tilton had been making a good run of it.

The ethics of the whole thing aside, Zizouzias was actually pretty pleased with himself.

DEL

Del Martin knew all about Tilton's hard-left convictions, and had been willing to go along with all of that for the sake of his personal ambition. That ambition was nowhere near the levels that Brock Tilton had gotten himself worked up to, but Del's visions of future glory were still on the robust side of large. He had no deep leftist principles to speak of, but he wasn't exactly against them either. Put simply, he was deeply committed to the future career and well-being of one Del Martin.

There is a certain kind of political intelligence—and it can be highly intelligent, as in this case—that for some reason is not connected with first principles. Del could follow the arguments, and he could cite the facts he had readily memorized in one sitting, and he was really good at anticipating what the other fellow was going to say. This was because the other fellow, whether from the left, right, or middle, rarely thought in terms of first principles either. And by *rarely*, it would be best to say that we mean *never*.

Tilton's first principles were almost entirely wrong and cockeyed, but they *were* first principles, and Tilton knew what they were, and he reasoned from them. Del was not in that position. He was willing to adapt to whatever Tilton was saying currently, and didn't even have to move that far to do it. And whatever distance he did have to move was fairly easy, because he didn't have to decouple from any first principles in order to make the shift.

So Del was personally ambitious, and that was the reality that overshadowed everything. He had grown up around the kind of soft left money that is characteristic of the big tech companies, and that had helped establish his factory settings. His father had gobs of that kind of money, and his mother had gobs of those sorts of politics, and they both were heavily invested in their son's future achievements. It would have been quite strange had Del gone in any other direction.

He had grown up in Cary, North Carolina, and gone off to college in Virginia, where he had decided to remain after graduation. He had gone to law school there, where he had met Gina, a native Virginian, who was a law student one year ahead of him. They had lived together for a few years and had then gotten married after he graduated.

After law school in Virginia, through some of Gina's family connections, which went back as far as James Madison on her mother's side, he was appointed to the Senate seat by the governor after his predecessor had blown up in a gaudy sex and cocaine spectacle. After two years of holding down the fort, he was elected easily and in his own right. With regard to the national stage, it was one of the easiest on-ramps imaginable. Del was ambitious, but he also felt as though fate was somehow in his corner, barking encouraging instructions at him between rounds. For the last few years he had felt like he was living in an invisible cloud of mojo.

As if to confirm this, the vice-presidential slot had come upon him from behind, and entirely unexpectedly. But he was the kind of person who was not averse to going through doors that opened to him suddenly in this fashion. That was how these things happened, was it not? He had been quite surprised when a representative from Tilton's vetting team had made an appointment with him, walked into his office one ten a.m., and told him that he was now on the veep short list, and that they would need his full cooperation if they were to go through all the things he had done back in college while not thinking of his future career. He had not been spotless, but he had been discrete, and that was good enough for them. After the brusque but not unfriendly phone call from Brock Tilton, Del had put his phone away and silently mouthed the inspired words uttered by Plunkitt of Tammany Hall a century and a half before. He had come across the quote while researching for a paper he had written in college. "I seen my opportunities and I took 'em."

Del was tall, but not outlandish about it, being just a couple inches over six feet. He looked older than he actually was, and had been graced with salt and pepper hair early on. This gave him the look of an energetic middle-aged man, instead of looking like a prematurely aged younger guy, which is what he was. As a candidate, he was attractive to women, and yet somehow not off-putting to men, no small accomplishment. He was a genuine quick study when it came to names. Whenever he was out on the rubber chicken circuit, and talking to some local functionary, Del knew how to connect with him, really *connect* with him, and how to make that man feel like the most important person in the world. He would learn that person's name, and he would *remember* that person's name, and he would use that remembered name to his advantage some time in the first six months after having learned it. He was good, almost Bill Clinton good.

Gina was a bright, attractive, soft-spoken woman. After they had married, she had at first gotten a job at a prestigious firm, and worked there for a couple of years before she got pregnant.

After their first boy was born, she moved to practicing law part-time until she discovered that she enjoyed the mothering part of her day far more than she enjoyed the legal part of her day. She had been staring at some briefs in her brief case, and then went into the laundry room and stared at some briefs in the laundry basket, and decided that work was work wherever you are, but that she preferred being with people she loved instead of being with people she didn't. So she gradually reduced her hours at the firm until the hours didn't register much anymore, had a heart-to-heart talk with Del, and just came home.

This was entirely a matter of personal preference. She was not making any social statement. Her upbringing had not been religious at all, and so that had played no part. What she had gleaned from her feminism was that she ought to be allowed to do what she wanted to do, and what she wanted to do was to be with her boys. The only surprise to her had been the reaction of some of the other women at the firm, a mixture of malice and envy. One day when one of the other attorneys had been particularly catty, and Gina was telling Del about it that night at dinner, Del had gotten pretty worked up about it, but Gina's only comment was that it "takes all kinds."

Marriage had been all right, mostly. She liked Del, but she really loved her boys.

ROCCO ENTERS THE PICTURE

Rocco Williamson was a "fixer," a doer of dirty deeds, but unlike the fellow in that old AC/DC song, such deeds did not come dirt cheap. A connoisseur of fine wines, a patron of Italian opera as performed by top talent in Italy, and a collector of ancient manuscripts, Rocco was, by turns, a hit man, an extortionist, a blackmailer, and anything else that might fit into that general category of coercive persuasion.

Rocco looked like the hobbyist part of his life, and not like the professional part of his life: a suave collector of the finer things. His name seemed to clash with all of that because Rocco sounded like he could have been named Bruiser or Bane, but it all made sense when you found out "Rocco" was just a nickname he had picked up in college. His given name was Rochester.

Rocco was slight, and dressed like he wanted to be almost dapper. He was meticulous about his appearance, but made sure that he didn't come across as compulsively fastidious. If a hair was out of place, it was out of place deliberately—and he made sure that one was usually out of place. He had decided years before that he would display the kind of impeccable taste that would tell all observers that he *could* have been perfectly impeccable if he had wanted to.

But what all of this meant was that his sources of income were not nearly as refined as his expenditures. He was responsible for a good third of the actual Clinton suicides. The number of the *actual* Clinton suicides was much lower than various conspiracy buffs would have it, but still, a lot higher than it ought to have been—higher than what is generally accepted.

More to our purposes, Brock Tilton had Rocco on retainer.

From all such facts, stated this baldly, it might be easy to assume that he had had something to do with the attempted hit on Dr. Helen Greene. But this would be a false assumption.

Had this been a true assumption, then Helen would have been a lot deader than she actually was.

When Steven Lee first realized that he had sent an entire batch of incriminating emails to Helen Greene, of all people, and his software confirmed that she had opened and read it, and that she had lied about it to him, he knew instantly what had to be done. He knew about the existence of the darker side of his political world, and he also knew some people who were tangentially involved in it. He didn't know a lot, but he did know the name of one person, a friend from law school, one Hugh Hasani, that he thought he could call. That friend had been turned down for a position at the UN, which is hard to accomplish, and in his bitterness he had become increasingly radical and impatient, a combination which came close to creating a perpetual motion machine of emotions. This Hugh was now the chief spokesman for a radical organization called Earth Fight.

Various writers and pundits on the right liked to call the Earth Fight contingent an eco-terror group, but the people within the group liked to describe themselves as simple believers in direct action. Defense of Mother Earth was actually self-defense, and they didn't care who knew it. Outside of the occasional Unabomber cabin, it would be hard to find people more committed to the purity of violence in pursuit of their goals than Earth Fight.

Their problem was that their expertise was limited to breaking shop windows in upscale urban shopping districts, setting cars on fire, and attacking VFW rallies, and then only when a lot of other people were doing the same thing. Even then they made sure that the veterans they attacked were from the Korean conflict and earlier.

They were more radical than antifa, but their commitment to radicalism had not yet translated into any kind of dogged commitment to excellence. That kind of thing seemed to them to smell suspiciously like work, and also to reflect a bourgeois mindset that they were trying to shake loose of, as it reminded them of their fathers, all of whom had been high functionaries and wheels in their local chambers of commerce. But their problem was that no matter how many Pottery Barn windows they smashed, their fathers were still important figures in their respective chambers of commerce. The thing seemed insoluble.

Their dedication to their cause meant that they were in principle ready to kill and maim for it, but their relativism as regards their work ethic meant that they were not really any good at killing and maiming. And it was, alas, this group that Steven Lee had (indirectly) dispatched to take care of his Helen Greene problem.

He had done this because Hugh had occasionally dropped some dark hints here and there about "what's really going down." And so when Steven outlined his problem, that problem being a colleague who had betrayed the cause, his friend had eagerly seized the opportunity. "Eve of destruction, baby," had been his one cryptic editorial comment. A much needed gift had been deposited in the account of Earth Fight, and Hugh told him to consider it done.

So Hugh was the one who had given the call to action to Maurice and Leon. He, like they, talked a serious game, for the future of the planet was at stake, and he, like they, was more or less a lummox, an oaf, and a simpleton. He thought that there wasn't a single problem on earth that wasn't directly related to the fact that mankind was pumping massive amounts of CO_2 into the *air*. In his world, temperatures had nothing to do with the fact that there was this huge globe of burning gas in the sky.

But now Hugh was the one who had to place a call to Steven Lee in order to inform him that Maurice was in the hospital, and under arrest, and that Leon was back at his mother's apartment, somewhat dispirited and in need of encouragement.

This threw Steven Lee into a high panic mode. He was normally a fairly steady scoundrel, not given to any emotional trapeze acts, but this thing was completely different. He knew that his life and career would be absolutely *done* if those emails even thought about coming out. He had it on good information he was going to be nominated for the Nobel this year, and a documentary telling the story of his life—*Lonely Hero*—was already in production for Netflix. He was all set to become a household name, and did not want to become a household name in any way other than the pathway-of-honors way.

But even his new found adrenaline levels were not bringing him any new information. He didn't know anybody he could call besides Hugh. Fortunately for Steven, Hugh's contacts were a little bit broader, and he had mentioned Rocco's name to Steven at the very end of Steven's most distressing phone call.

Steven called the number right away, introduced himself, and waded in from the shallow end. He started by saying that he was an old acquaintance of Hugh Hasani, and had contracted with him to take care of a little business . . .

Rocco interrupted him. "So that's why that Maurice clown is in the hospital! Up and coming climate scientist disappears into the morning mist mysteriously, and one of Hugh's Neanderthals is found bleeding on her carpet! I thank you heartily for the missing piece. I have been puzzling over it all morning."

Steven breathed a sigh of relief. He didn't want to play any games anyhow.

"What is, um, your fee structure?" He said. "I know that this botch means that I am not in a strong negotiating position."

"No, no, you are not," Rocco said, and named his fee. "But in addition to that fee, I also demand a free hand. I never leave any loose ends lying around."

"What do you mean?" Steven asked.

"I mean Maurice, and Leon, and maybe Hugh."

Steven felt he could hear the cry of pain from his checking account, but had gotten up that morning early and read through the whole chain of emails again, just to make sure. "Yes," he said. "Just do what you need to, and it is good to work with a professional."

CHAPTER 3

Gassing Up

LARRY LOCKE

Larry Locke did not look at all like a successful author. In his late twenties now, he had made most of his living as a logger in Montana. He had started at that when he was sixteen, and worked around his school schedule, and had done the same through college. He had managed to work full time, and graduate on time. And his looks belied him. He was six foot ten, and about three hundred pounds of hardened muscle. That wasn't the part that belied him because he *looked* like a logger from Montana. He was also a wolf and bear hunter, and he looked like those two things also.

It was the *successful author* part that threw people. Four years before, he had walked into the D.C. offices of Aegis Imprint, and plopped a manuscript down on the desk of the receptionist. He had asked her, very politely, how these things were usually handled, and who he should show his manuscript to. The receptionist, normally very adept at handling walk-ins who knew they were supposed to be big time successful authors, was freaked out by Larry's size, not to mention his apparent outlook on life. She squeaked something like "excuse me," and darted into the office behind her, that office belonging to Ken Corcharan.

He was the founder, owner, and publisher of Aegis Imprint, a wildly successful publisher of inflammatory conservative books and magazines. He was a hard case, with a straight-line edge, but not a sociopath. That said, if he ever got bitten by a diamondback, the snake would be the one that died. At the same time, he was a shrewd judge of horseflesh, so to speak, which is how he got to the place where he was. When we refer to him as a hard case, we are talking about his demeanor toward competitors, not toward his authors. He was astonishingly generous to his authors.

In fact, he was asked about that once in an interview with *Publishers Weekly*, and he said that the normal practices of the publishing industry seemed to him to border on the insane. "Publishers cozy up to their social peers among the competition, and schmooze around like there is no tomorrow, and then turn around and treat their authors like *they* were the competition. But if I were the owner of racehorses, I wouldn't be chumming around with owners of other horses, who wanted me and my horse dead, but until that glad day arrived would willingly invite me to their parties on Martha's

Vineyard. And then to compensate for such lunacy, would I feed all my horses on cheap oats?" This parable was a dark saying for most readers of *Publishers Weekly*, except for the authors. The authors liked it.

But meanwhile, back at Aegis Imprint, the receptionist, whose name was Mindi, was pleading with Ken to come out and handle this one. *Please.*

And so it was that Ken came out, shook Larry's hand, and said *pleased-to-meetcher*, and told Larry that he did have fifteen minutes to spare, and to come right in. Larry picked the manuscript up from the receptionist's desk and brought it in with him, and plonked it right in front of where Ken usually sat. He didn't even have to bend over to reach across the desk.

Ken had looked at the title page, which read, simply, *Ecochondriacs*. He flipped over a few pages until he got to the introduction and read the first three paragraphs, at the end of which he fully came to grips with the discordant note that was being struck somewhere in his brain.

The man sitting in front of him was a total unit, like two or three Navy SEALS packed into one. Moreover, he *looked* like a logger, the kind that could walk out of the woods with a tree under each arm. And yet . . .

"You write this yourself?" Ken asked.

Larry had nodded. "Yes. Yes, I did."

The prose read like it had been written by the archangel Gabriel—when the muse was on him, when he was writing hot, and was going real good. Ken sat back in his chair, and stared at Larry for a moment. Then he stared for two moments.

"Look," he said, leaning forward. "This is not how it happens. This never happens. It doesn't work this way. Don't tell anybody about it. But you have yourself a book deal."

But it turned out that those three paragraphs that Ken was gambling on were actually kind of pedestrian compared to later passages in the book. Larry had a huge gift for making complicated issues plain, and to do so without distorting what the actual issues were. He wrote intelligently and with verve. He wrote with authority, and not as the scribblers.

And that is how his book had made it into the stratosphere of book sales. It was the most successful book that Aegis had ever published, which was saying something, and it even elbowed its way to the top of the New York Times bestseller list, and was still, a few years later, bouncing along at the top of the Amazon rankings.

As a consequence of all this, Larry had found himself with more money than he knew what to do with. *That* had lasted for about three months, after which he figured out through some hard thinking what he was going to do with it all. He was a quick study when it came to piles of money, and those close to him were all pleased that it did not go to his head, not even a little bit. He bought a remote lakeside cabin back in western Montana, free and clear, on a 140-acre parcel in the mountains. That was where he was going to live, and fish, and hunt, and write some more great literature. He was going to do his part to save Western Civilization, but he was going to do it with a backdrop of gorgeous mountains. Why not? he thought. Calvin wrote his commentaries with the Alps right *there*.

But he also bought two pieces of property in the D.C. area. One was a condominium, a place to hang his hat while trying to talk sense into congressmen, which was a strenuous activity in its own right, and the other was a medium-sized office complex on ten acres. This latter property was the headquarters of Ecosense, an organization dedicated to the restoration of ecological sanity. And the founder and president of this entity was Larry Locke himself. He defined ecological sanity as a world that didn't have any environmentalists in it anymore, except three at the South Pole perhaps, studying the weather. Not the climate, but the weather.

The name Ecosense initially gave visitors a warm glow, the kind you get when dealing with reasonable conservatives, the kind who are quietly selling the farm while trying to keep Grandma, sitting there in the front parlor, reassured that nothing like that could ever happen to the family dairy that we all hold so dear. But when you drove up and parked in the front lot of this particular organization called Ecosense, you started to get a different vibe. Or you did as soon as you got out of your car.

The first thing that struck you was the fact that there was a large pillar right behind the flagpole on the large, grassy circle that you had to drive around to drop someone off at the front door. On top of this stout pillar, about fifteen feet up, was a stretch Hummer, jet black. If you went and stood by the base of it, you could hear that the Hummer was running. It was running all day and all night, virtually all the time. Part of the maintenance man's night shift duties was to come out at four a.m. and turn it off for a half-hour respite, gas it up, and have it going again by six when the first staff workers started arriving.

"We don't know how long that beast can go," Larry said. "But we will find out. And then when it konks, we will just have to get a new one."

"But . . . but *why?*" A reporter had once asked, querulously.

"Because CO_2 helps keep the vegetation green. We are a green organization all the way, baby. I mean, look at those bushes over there. That hot Hummer air is mother's milk to them." Larry had replied. And he had said no more about it.

Ecosense was an organization filled to the rafters with eco-resistance radicals. And by eco-resistance, I mean resistance *to* the environmentalists, and not resistance to those evil corporations that go out and find the fossil fuels that keep us all happy and warm. And by rafters, I mean the laminated kind that were put together in a big factory using a lot of industrial glue. It was a special point of pride for Larry, and he would point those rafters out to visitors.

The second indication that this organization was serious business was the informal mission and vision statement of Ecosense, the one emblazoned on the wall right behind the reception desk, right under the stylized logo and the word *Ecosense.* That mission statement was, "To fight the pagan death cult until we hang their last dog."

THIS SAME LARRY

This very same Larry was walking across the parking lot toward the offices of Aegis Imprint again. He visited Ken more often now that he lived half the year in the D.C. area, and he enjoyed the visits. It was one of the few things in D.C. that he did enjoy. Larry was probably one of three people on the planet who was not in the least intimidated by Ken, and this was something that Ken enjoyed twice as much as he would admit to himself.

Larry would occasionally come by just to shoot the breeze, but this visit had a purpose. Ken had been after him to write a follow-up volume to *Ecochondriacs*, and Larry had just had the idea for the hook two days before. He didn't want to write anything until he thought he had something worthwhile to say, and now he thought he did. He stuck up a yellow post-it note somewhere in his brain reminding him to drop in on Aegis some time that week. And then he had gotten a one-word email from Ken yesterday, summoning him. *C'mere*, the email had said. And so here he was, ready to both listen and speak.

Mindi the receptionist was more or less used to Larry by this point, but despite her best efforts she still would go a little pale whenever he would appear, which she did once again this morning. But she quickly got command of herself and buzzed through to Ken while Larry was still navigating through the double doors, which given his size and the size of the doors was something of a production, and which gave Ken the opportunity to bring his phone conversation in for a landing.

As Larry approached the reception desk, Ken suddenly appeared in his doorway. "Larry! Prince among authors! Come in, come in."

Larry did so, closed the door behind him, and when they were seated, he said. "You've got something, and I've got something. Who first?"

"You first," Ken said, gallantly.

And so Larry pitched the hook for his next book, filled it out a little bit, and then sat back and waited.

"Well?" he said after a moment.

Ken was busy chewing on his pen, which he pulled out and stared at as though it were a fine cigar that wasn't pulling properly. "It is like this, Larry," he said. "Your idea for a sequel could be terrible, and *Ecochondriacs* was so good that the follow-up will still sell a million copies. The third one might not, but the second one would. That is why I have been hounding you for the last year. That is how it would sell if it was *terrible*, and your idea sounds pretty good. How you learned how to type with those bratwurst fingers of yours beats me. But you figured out how to do it, and last time you gave me some of the most lucid prose I have ever seen. Next time around could be half as good, and still be really good. So count me in."

"Great," Larry said. "I'll get it organized, and I might even get started. What was your thing?"

"Do you know your junior senator from Montana? Like, at all?"

"I have met her twice. Once at a hotel chicken event in Bozeman, with some speeches bad enough to make your back teeth ache. Hers was not like that, and was actually pretty good. Wish she would vote as good as she talked. The other time I met her was at a much gaudier event here in D.C.. She was pleasant enough, even knowing who I was, but as you know, on environmental issues, she is not my dream gal."

Sen. Marsha Hart was the aforementioned junior senator from Montana, a solid Republican and a wobbly conservative.

She managed to keep her overall reputation as a mild right-of-center conservative, but she had also been known to let the side down on certain key votes.

Larry continued. "I have talked to a few of those lobbyists, those K Street konservatives, and they are happy enough with her because on *their* issues I suppose she is conservative enough. But she has been really bad on environmental stuff. Really bad. I don't get it."

"Well, here," Ken said, "is where I come in. I can increase your storehouse of knowledge. She would actually be happy to vote with the good guys all the time, and that would actually make her campaigning back in Montana a lot simpler for her. It is as tricky as it is because—I have sources—the FBI had some dirt on her that was related to her first marriage and some business deals related to all of that, which in the last two Obama years, found its way into the hands of certain Democratic operatives. They use it to apply just the right amount of pressure to her from time to time. Not so much that they would wreck her ACU national ranking, which might actually threaten her re-election. Whoever these guys are, they are playing it shrewd. They only flex when the vote has to do with the environment, and then only half the time. "

"Huh," Larry responded.

"You know," Ken said, "whenever some politician's behavior—and I include Supreme Court justices in that category of politician—seems utterly inexplicable, Occam's razor would tell us to start our first line of questioning at whether or not there are incriminating photos of said politician during his college years. That's the only thing I can think of that would explain some of John Roberts' legal reasoning. And given the caliber of *that* reasoning, I would have to infer that the photos are of him leaning away from a stripper pole with a basket of fruit on his head."

Larry grinned and acknowledged receipt of the image with a nod, and then said, "I know. This is a sad town, full of sad stories. But what does any of this have to do with me?"

"Well, aren't you the radical-right enviro meet-and-greet guy? I think you should make an appointment and go see her."

"Ken," Larry said, leaning forward in his chair, which made it start to creak more than a little bit. "There was a whole *chapter* on her pipeline flake in my book. I don't think that *she* thinks that what her day at the office needs is a little visit from Larry Locke."

"You are from Montana, and you are now a big wheel on environmental issues for the right. The biggest wheel, I might add, thanks to your way with adjectives and prose that shines like a mountain lake by moonlight. You being so darn *big* also helps. She is a senator from Montana. You just drop in, allude to that chapter in a manly way, saying that it was nothing personal. And that if there is ever anything you can do for her, she can feel free to ask."

"All right," Larry growled. "The mission is clear enough, and apparently innocent enough. But why? What are you up to? Why don't *you* go?"

"I ran her publisher clean into bankruptcy about three weeks after her book with them released. It was supposed to be their event of the season, and subsequent events proved that this was not to be the case. You suspect you might not be welcome there. I *know* that I will not be."

"Okay, that's why not you. Why me? Why anybody?"

"Those mysterious sources I mentioned earlier? One of them was an exotic beauty with a strange accent, a black veil, and a pearl-handled derringer. She told me that she thought Hart is being worked over by some of the bad guys. I had another place I could check, and they confirmed it, or at least said it was a likely possibility."

"Well," Larry said, "I can believe it, except for the exotic beauty part. That's how this town operates, right? What good would it do for me to go shake her hand?"

Ken leaned forward in his chair. "Just do your normal routine, the way you go around the capitol to meet the swells. If she is friendly to you, of *all* people, then she might be open to some of our people throwing her a rope. Not that we have a rope to throw, just yet. But it might motivate some of us to go look for a rope."

Larry was dubious. "I still don't see the point. But part of my task here in this awful town was to go meet all the senators that would be willing to see me. All I need to do is move her up on the list. But only because you asked me sweetly."

"I did, didn't I?" Ken said.

GINA IS TIRED OF IT

Meanwhile Gina Martin sat down on the couch again, after having walked back and forth across the room several times.

She wasn't nervous, or afraid. It was just that she *hated* conflict, and she had finally settled in her mind that she was going to have herself some conflict anyhow. That is why she had a margarita in her hand, even though it wasn't dinner time yet, and that was why she took another sip of it. She was the kind of woman who wouldn't get into a conflict unless she was going to win it, and yet she was kind-hearted enough to hate whatever damage was done to others in the course of winning it.

She heard Del in the foyer, taking off his coat and hanging up his satchel, and so she just sat there, glass in hand. Here it comes. The kids were at her mother's for the weekend, and so it would be just the two of them. He came into the living room, rubbing his hands. He had had, from all initial appearances, a good day. He had texted when he hit the freeway, and he was within a couple of minutes of his predicted time, and so a margarita was waiting by his chair for him. There was nothing in the welcoming set up to indicate to him that Gina was about to tell him that she was going to file for divorce right after the election.

But she was, and when he sat down, she got right to the point. She was businesslike, and even affable at times, but all the necessary firmness was there. If ever a woman had *had* it with someone else's cheating ways, this woman was in that category.

"Del, I found out about Kara today." Kara was a low-level staffer on the campaign. Gina had only met her twice, and had thought her entirely too slinky on first acquaintance. When she met her the second time she had thought her slinkier. A phrase she had once read in Wodehouse had come to mind—a snake with hips.

When she said this, Del twitched, startled, and sat up straight in his chair. He didn't protest, but it looked as though he was thinking about it, and so Gina held up her hand. "I don't want to argue about it, or inquire into it, or waste any time talking about it. Just know that I know, and that my intelligence is really good."

He knew he was caught, fair and square. So Del sat back, waiting for the blast. In their fifteen years of marriage, he had strayed a total of five times. Gina had found out about three of them, counting this time with Kara, and each of the previous two times had been followed by a fierce argument, filled with recriminations, accusations, and sobs. So Del sat back, waiting for her to begin, and braced himself for it. If he just weathered the storm, things would get back to normal eventually.

But what she did was astonish him. She said, in calm and measured tones, "Del, I don't know what it is. I don't even pretend to understand it. You are very nice to me in every other way. We *like* each other. So I know that you are not trying to hurt me intentionally. But you do it anyway, and so I have decided that it is well past time for me to move out of range. And by that, I mean *completely* out of range."

That startled him again, but differently, and he sat up straighter again. He went a little pale around the lips, which she noticed.

"What . . . what do you mean?" he faltered.

"After I received my intelligence report this morning, I spent a lot of time thinking about it. And what I wanted to do tonight is explain to you how the divorce is going to happen."

"Divorce?" He had no right to be amazed at the prospect of divorce appearing suddenly like this, but it is often the case that delusional people experience feelings that they have no right to experience. "*Divorce?*" he said again.

"Yes," she said. "And this is how it is going to happen. I have no desire to destroy your career, or mess anything up for you, now that everything is going so well for you. The vice-presidential nomination and all."

He nodded, still stunned. As alluded to earlier, he had no right to be stunned, but that didn't keep him from being stunned.

"I am not going to file until the week after the election. I am willing to make all the campaign appearances you need, and everything stays normal that way. As far as anybody else in the world is concerned, we are married until the election. Then we will be divorced. If you win the election, my leaving will be at the beginning of a four-year-term, and I will be ancient history by the time the next election comes around. If you lose the election, nobody will care, and I will not have destroyed anything for you. And you will still have your Senate seat."

He had slumped in his chair, and after a few minutes gestured helplessly. "But what about now, between now and the election?"

"I am not sure what you are asking, precisely, but if we are here by ourselves, and not on some campaign stage, then you should consider us to be already divorced. We are done. I do think we should endeavor to be civil and civilized, for the boys' sake, but apart from the legal work we are already *done*. As done as it gets."

"Where will I sleep? . . . the boys will notice . . ."

"In our bedroom, just so the boys don't ask questions. I will explain it all to them after the election. But no sex, and no sly attempts at it either. That won't fix anything."

"But I don't want a divorce," he finally said.

"Yes, but I do. And I am the one who is getting one."

"I . . . I don't want a divorce," he said again.

"But you clearly don't want to be married to *me* either."

He had no comeback for that one, so he went back to an earlier point. He said, "You said earlier that 'everything is working out for me.' But everything is actually working out for *us*. It's all coming together, babe."

"Not any more," she said with finality. "Not any more."

"Babe, don't be hasty. You could be First Lady some day . . ."

"I know that I could. And I know that I would be just as miserable as some of our other First Ladies have been. I would much prefer the exclusion of all second ladies than to be First Lady."

"But . . ."

She held up her hand gracefully, and even somewhat graciously, but still imperiously. "*Done,*" she said.

ACCIDENTAL GOSPEL

Montenegro Cash was the kind of television evangelist who sincerely believed in milking the faithful, which is what he faithfully did. Whatever negative stereotypes the reader might have picked up about televangelists, in this case they were not stereotypes at all—they were basically true. This one had no personal faith in God at all, but he did have a great deal of personal charisma. If he had not gone into the ministry, he would have gone into the musical entertainment industry, and would have done very well there, and for all the same reasons.

He was gifted and glib, he was smart and sassy, and he was telegenic. His smile had to be seen to be believed, and he could sell just about anything to just about anybody. The product that he always had the most success with was his ability to sell *himself* from virtually any stage in the world. He was a settled atheist, but one of the things he had decided early on was to never tell anybody about *that*. If there was no God, then he was going to look out for old number one. And in the circles he was going to be traveling in, saying that there was no God was not the way to get ahead with anybody. Why alienate most of the potential customers and consumers in the world, right off the bat?

Montenegro had to deliver biblical messages all the time, every night, and so he was on the clock constantly, but couldn't be bothered to read or study the Bible for himself—he was a busy man. But he had a staff of three writers who were smart enough to read and believe what they were reading, but who were also—if we are being frank here—goobers of unbounded and amiable gullibility. They knew just the kind of thing that Montenegro wanted them to extract from the text, and so extract it they did. And they believed all of it, too.

One time they had given him a little monologue, which he had delivered straight to camera, which argued that if you divided the name *Adam* into two words, *a dam*, you could see how easy it was for our humanity to become a blockage to the divine energy. If you wanted the energy to *flow*, you really needed to blow up that dam. It had occurred to Montenegro while he was delivering this particular message that this also had the added blessing of freeing up all the spiritual salmon, but he didn't say anything about that.

Montenegro was quite successful at what he did, but not so successful that he could get his show out of the middle of the night yet, the place where it was currently stuck. But breaking out into the big time was just a matter of time, Montenegro knew. As for the present, when he was musing philosophically about it, his current time slot was probably all for the best—because the kind of thing he was selling might not work that well in the broad daylight. When it was time for him to make his move, he could gradually modify his message.

One of his staff writers had gotten pregnant about a year before all this, and had had the baby about three months back. The original plan had been for her to return after her maternity leave was complete. But she had discovered, after about a week home with her baby, that she *adored* her baby. In fact, as she said to herself, about a week after that, she loved her baby significantly more than she loved her job. Two weeks later, when the baby had started to do *amazing* things like gurgle in adorable ways, she told her husband that she loved being a mom far more than she liked writing piffle for Montenegro Cash. This led to quite a fruitful conversation with her husband, who had been calling it piffle under his breath for a while already. And so she gave her notice, which started a chain of events in their lives that resulted in them joining a local evangelical Presbyterian church and disappearing from our story.

This is only mentioned because this created a sudden and unexpected job opening at Montenegro's studio, and in the rush to get somebody, they accidentally hired someone who had an actual supply of actual Bible knowledge. This young man's name was Owen Swallow, and he had actually attended a classical Christian school in Baltimore. He was whip smart without being whip wise, which meant that he had far more biblical knowledge at his fingertips than the usual staff writer there at the studio had, meaning that there were fewer Wikipedia rabbit-hole searches, but it also meant that he was clueless enough about what was going on in the ministry of Montenegro Cash to not struggle with any conscience-ridden sleepless nights.

Owen had been working there for about a week when he was thrown onto his own devices. Both of his experienced co-workers came down with a virulent flu, and so Owen had to produce something for that night's monologue all by himself. He had learned the ropes well enough to know what the word count needed to be, and what the cadences needed to be like, but he had not mastered the entire groove yet. And so, in that "think fast" moment, he retreated to all the chapel presentations he had ever heard, which was a pretty large number, which in turn meant that a good deal of actual gospel got into the monologue.

This resulted in Montenegro Cash saying *what the hell* to himself several times while delivering that particular monologue, and making a mental note to have somebody talk to the new guy. Be that as it may, he still delivered what was on the teleprompter—no time for a rewrite—and he delivered it with his usual panache and aplomb and charisma, and all of it wreathed in radiant smiles.

MONTENEGRO GETS TO DEL

Del had left the house, furious that Gina had refused to fight with him over Kara. Whenever they had had their previous fights over his affairs, the arguments had rapidly descended to an ugly level, at which level both of them said a number of unkind things about the other person, and Del had gotten into the habit of using any cruel things that Gina had said as a form of retroactive justification for anything he might have said or done prior to that point.

In other words, his adulteries were unprovoked, but in the fights over them afterwards, he could always act like they were somehow provoked by Gina's subsequent reaction. Entirely irrational, of course, but Del had somehow missed that this was a technique of his until that mysterious moment when Gina had refused to do or say anything cruel, unkind, mean, or vindictive. She had been entirely reasonable the entire time, and she did not say or do anything that would enable him to justify any of his trysts with Kara. She just left him hanging out to dry, in other words.

But while she was reasonable, she was also adamant. They were *going* to be divorced. She refused to blow up the campaign, but if he won national office, as it very much looked like he might, she would not be there with him. And neither would Kara be there. Kara was a low-level staff twinkie. *She* didn't belong on a national stage.

Gina did. She was a natural. Del respected her, looked up to her, and actually thought that he loved her. But at the moment he was furious with her for not allowing him to play his usual games. That left him with nothing but guilt, and the unpleasant sensation of being the moral equivalent of a three-inch green tree frog. It was not a sensation he was accustomed to, and he did not like it, not one little bit.

He drove angrily to a nearby hotel, one that was near the airport. He sometimes stayed there when he had an early morning flight, and they would just assume that such was the case here. He had an emergency travel kit in the trunk, so he was good there. He felt momentarily bad about the Secret Service guy who had to follow him out there, but that is what they were paid for. Normally in the evenings it was a fellow named Bert, but this time it was an agent named Keith. He seemed fully capable of not asking awkward questions, for which Del was grateful.

The car jerked to a stop in the hotel parking lot, and Del stomped across the parking lot, kicking a few small stones as he went. He checked in, glowering at the pleasant young lady behind the desk, went to his room, threw the travel kit on the bed, and then went down to the hotel restaurant to order a steak and a beer. It soon came, sizzling hot, and any other patron of the restaurant would have praised it to the skies. It could have been shoe leather for all Del noticed. He cut and ate mechanically, downed the beer, and went back up to his room.

It was late, but Del took a long hot shower, hoping that it would relax his shoulders, which were as tight as they had been in years. That done, he staggered to the bed and collapsed. And his strategy *almost* worked. He slept like a sunken and deeply saturated log . . . for about four hours. And then, in the middle of the night, suddenly, his eyes popped wide open. He was awake, and he knew instantly that he was *awake* awake. He stared at the ceiling for about fifteen minutes, weighing his options.

After a fruitless little bit of that, he got up, sat in the desk chair, and flipped on the television. He flipped through the channels listlessly, wondering what there could be broadcasting out there in the middle of the night that could possibly occupy his mind. In pursuit of this form of a flickering anodyne, he came upon a screen full of bacchanalian pornography, which he watched for about five minutes. Then he said *gaaahh!* and flipped the channel again.

And when he did so, he found himself immediately confronted by the energetic and very charismatic figure of Montenegro Cash. He started feeling around for the button that would rid him of this televangelical pestilence, but then something stopped him. He didn't know what it was, but whatever it was *stopped* him. In the flickering light of the screen, he looked down, made sure he had the right button, and pointed the remote at the television. *No*, a voice said, right behind him.

Del uttered an expletive, dropped the remote, and jumped out of his chair, whirling around as he did so. Nobody there. He picked up the remote again, and pointed it at the television again. This time the voice came again, it seemed from the bathroom. *No*, it said again. This time, he set the remote carefully on the bed, and walked cautiously to the bathroom and flicked on the light. Nobody there.

While he was thus occupied, Montenegro Cash had been busy selling little vials of water, taken from the Jordan River, "where our Lord was baptized." Had Del watched any of that spiel, it is doubtful that it would have done him any spiritual good at all. He would have been too busy speculating that the water in those vials probably came from the faucets in the bathrooms of Montenegro Cash's studio, which in fact they had.

But by the time he returned, that particular sales pitch was over, and the evangelist was moving seamlessly into his monologue. And right about the time that Montenegro Cash was thinking his very first *what the hell*, Del was sitting on the edge of his bed, entranced. Everything about this made sense. And by the time Montenegro got to his second *what the hell*, Del was wavering. It made too much sense. And at the conclusion of the monologue, in the final paragraph, Montenegro said, straight to camera, with oceanic concern in his eyes, "Maybe you are sitting alone in a hotel room. Your wife has just said she wants a divorce. You know her request is entirely fair. You know just what you need to do. You need Jesus."

This was right before Montenegro's third *what the hell*, but Del didn't get that far. He flipped the television off, this time with no opposition from his invisible friend, set the remote next to the television set, and took three deep breaths. He was standing there in his skivvies, with his feet kind of cold by this point, but slowly, deliberately, knowing full well what he was doing, he got down on his knees and repented.

He started with this most recent adultery, and then moved on to the others that Gina had found out about. After that he repented of the affairs that Gina did not know about. When he was done with adultery, he moved on to his lying. He had been a most shameless liar. Systematically, he found himself repenting of a good deal of the infrastructure of his entire life. And as he was dropping all these various sins to the ground, he found that he had in fact been carrying them all for years. Once they were gone, he started to notice how heavy they had been.

Some of them fell noiselessly. Some of them clattered. Some of them felt as though they just floated away. He stayed on his knees that way, repenting of a life filled to the rim with sham and pretense and politics, for about forty-five minutes.

He felt instinctively that he needed to do something else. He felt enormously relieved in what he was doing, but he still felt as though it needed closure. This was grand and all, but it needed a lid. He couldn't just repent all night. And for some reason a phrase floated into his memory from a Bible as lit course he had taken as a sophomore in college. That class had been a joke and a half, taught by an alcoholic and semi-retired United Methodist minister who didn't believe in *anything*. But a phrase came back to Del from across the years from that class, that phrase being *repent and believe*. When he remembered that, he paired it up with what Montenegro Cash had just said about coming to Jesus. And so Del did. He came to Jesus.

"Jesus," he said, "I know I am probably doing this all wrong. But if you will have me, please take me. Damn it, I'm here."

CHAPTER 4

The Crying Need for Revolution

MEETING THE SENATOR

Jill Stevens had gotten a ride to work from Shelly, her next door neighbor, because her new employee (and perhaps new friend) Eve and her husband Trevor—Jill hadn't met him yet— were going to take her out to dinner that night. Eve said that they could easily drop her off at her condo on their way home afterwards, as it was right on the way.

Work, as it happened, was at the Senate Office Building in Washington, D.C. Jill was a senior staffer for the junior senator from Montana, and had been there for a few years now. She loved her job, actually, and she also loved going briskly up the stairs, which she was now doing.

She was just a quarter-inch shy of six feet tall, which had made her a natural wing spiker for her high-school volleyball

53

team, and then also for four years at college, the last two of which were championship years. When she was in eighth grade, the time when it had first become apparent that she was going to be six feet tall, or something very much like it, her father had taken her out on a date, and solemnly charged her to own it. "This is God's gift to you. Lean into it. *Own* it," he had said. She always looked back on that date as a turning point in her life, and it was the reason why she was wearing heels now.

On top of everything else, she was a striking blonde, which when combined with her height, made it easy to see her a long way off, even down a very crowded hallway.

A few moments later, she got off a jammed elevator, and made her way to the senator's office. She was five minutes early, which was, according to her punctual personality, five minutes late, and Eve had apparently beaten her by a skinny minute. Eve was already sitting at her reception desk, where Jill greeted her as she walked her purse back to her office, and then came back out to chat for a minute. Jill and Eve had hit it off instantly when they had first met, which is the reason Jill had hired her.

That day, like most of their days, was filled with an alternating pattern—first surges of humanity, and then, as though a hidden somebody had given a signal, absolutely no one. That afternoon, during one of those "no one" spots, Eve stopped her when Jill was walking back to the office. "Trevor has the day off, and so he is doing his specialty smoker/barbecue thing for us. I don't know what it is he does with that thing, but the results are magical. I am putting together the side dishes. I should have checked earlier, but do you have any allergies?" Jill shook her head *no*, and so she was standing there chatting easily about how her father used to smoke tri-tip too.

Actually, it looked like they were chatting easily, but Jill was nevertheless on her guard. A few days before this, when the two women had been chatting in just this same way, Eve had asked if she was seeing anyone.

"No, no," Jill had said. "Nothing against it, I suppose. But the pickings are pretty slim around here, you must admit. And I do have something of a prejudice against dating someone if I thought I could beat him up in a fair fight."

Eve had laughed at that, but Jill was still a bit wary now. She might bring it up again, and it was not Jill's most comfortable topic. She started to feel a sense of mild panic. *Maybe they asked her to come to dinner that night so they could try to set her up with an ugly cousin or something.*

But as they were talking this time, Jill suddenly saw a shadow fall across the desk and a second later she saw Eve's eyes get a little wider. "Wha . . .?" she said, and turned around. She stood there silently, as she watched the largest man she thought she had ever seen bow his head to come through the door. She had seen men that *tall* before, but never a man that tall who wasn't a bean pole.

He was beyond solid, and well proportioned. He looked like Achilles in the middle of an extended Homeric simile. But unlike Achilles, he was wearing slacks and suit jacket, but no tie. His beard was of a medium length, and almost yellow. His hair was a little darker, and Jill swallowed hard. He shifted his tablet to his left hand, and shook the hand that Jill had extended. For the first time in her life, Jill felt understated and diminutive. But she then took her courage in both hands, and spoke up like everything was normal.

"My name is Jill Stevens, assistant to Senator Hart. How can I help you?"

"Larry Locke. I believe I have a two o'clock with the senator."

Jill had been an assistant to the good senator from Montana for the last three years. She was a native of Baltimore, and was an ardent conservative, making her a good deal more conservative than her boss's voting record might have indicated. But the discrepancy was not so great as to cause her a crisis of conscience, at least not yet.

"Larry Locke? Not the author of *Ecochondriacs*?"

"The same guy. But I do not ask that people love it. It is enough for me that they have simply heard of it, and so you have made me happy already."

Eve, who was currently reading that very same book on her lunch breaks, had swiftly retrieved her copy from her purse, and slid it open across her desk with a pen on top of it. Larry obligingly stepped over and signed it quickly while Jill had started to head off down the hall. She came back after just a moment, and said, "The senator is finishing a phone call. It should less than five minutes, and many apologies."

Larry nodded affably, and Jill invited him to take a seat in the corner of the office where there were a couple of chairs of the sort you find in waiting rooms. There was an end table between them with a small stack of *National Reviews* in a tasteful spread, with a large rubber plant behind the end table. Larry took a seat and, overshadowed by the rubber plant, became as inconspicuous as it is possible for a man of his size to be.

And at just that moment, there was a clatter and a rustle and pother of self-importance at the door of the office, and three women, of the protesting variety, came in. Larry sat up a little straighter, putting down his magazine. He thought he was detecting the approach of something interesting. *He* was interested at any rate.

Jill was used to this kind of protestor, while Eve, who had only been in the office for a few months, was not. Jill caught Eve's eye, as much as to say that she would be happy to handle it. *Thanks much*, Eve thought back at her.

Of the three women, the one who was out in front and apparently the spokesman for them all could have been attractive if she had wanted to be, or she used to be attractive, or something of that nature. The other two were in a different category entirely. *They* looked like nothing on earth.

"We are here to speak with the senator about her support for the IRS education voucher bill . . ."

"I am sorry," Jill said sweetly. "Do you have an appointment?" She had just looked at the calendar ten minutes before. They didn't have an appointment.

"We don't need an appointment. We are here on the people's business."

"Well, being on the people's business won't help you if the senator is going to be on the floor of the Senate all the rest of the afternoon. If you really wanted to see her, the thing to do is to schedule an appointment. What organization do you represent?"

The spokesman turned away in fake wrath, the pique of a toddler unaccustomed to being crossed. "I don't need to represent *any* organization. My name is Marcie, and I want to be a witness in the hearing about that bill, if you have one. I am a *graduate* of one of those crappy Christian schools . . ."

Jill interrupted her, brightly. "Why, so am I!"

"Well, I don't believe in your God anymore," Marcie said in a *take that* sort of way. "And the reason why I don't believe in God is that the science teacher at that hellhole of a school groomed me for my whole junior year, and had his way with me for my whole senior year. What do you make of that, oh loyal alumnus? There is no God," she said with finality.

"There is no God?" Jill asked.

"*You* heard me." And then, remembering why they had come, she added, "And that is why any kind of tax credit for those places is unconscionable. I find it scarcely credible that anyone from *this* century would have proposed it. And as a native of Helena, I would like to testify."

"But if there is no God," Jill said, returning to the earlier theme, "what could possibly be wrong with what your science teacher did?" Jill had taken an apologetics class her senior year, apparently spending that final year more productively than her interlocutor.

"*What*?" her interlocutor said.

"I said that if there is no God, and if mores are defined by society, and provided he didn't get caught—he didn't get caught, did he?—there is no problem with what he did."

"You can't be serious . . ."

"Oh, deadly serious. No God, above us, only sky. It seems that boinking nubile young dopes would be just the ticket. If morality is just a social construct, one has to admire that kind of clear-headed behavior. And in a Christian school, too."

Marcie just stared. Jill looked back at her with her very best fat face. And, as fat faces go, it was a pretty good one.

Marcie was rummaging around in her mind, trying to think of a clever comeback, but couldn't come up with one and had to settle for something she remembered from fifth grade. "What makes *you* so smart?"

"I studied. And I did my senior thesis at *my* classical Christian school on morality and the existence of God. Instead of boinking any of the teachers."

Marcie stared some more, completely unused to this sort of thing.

"Would you like to make an appointment with the senator?"

Marcie shook her head curtly. *No*, she said, for emphasis. The other two preceded her, and she tried to slam the door after going out, but they were the sort of doors that would not slam. The effect was anti-climactic in the extreme.

The three women disappeared down the hallway to the right. "*Well*," Eve said.

Larry laughed out loud in the corner. "Well, that made *my* day," he said.

Jill flushed, and disappeared down the hall to check on the senator's phone call.

Reappearing just moment later, she said, "The senator's office is this way." Larry jumped to his feet to follow her, and

Eve noticed how quick and cat-like he was. Big cat. But when he disappeared from her line of sight, she cocked an ear for a moment. There was no indication, faint or loud, of anything like *fee fi fo fum*.

Jill came out just a few minutes later, having made the introduction, and having obtained a small bottle of water for Larry and also for the senator. "Well, the introduction went off well enough," she said.

"I know," Eve said. "I think I know why you might think that it wouldn't have. I just completed the chapter where he finished off our dear senator from Montana. Whatever would bring him *here*?"

They speculated about that for a few moments, and then returned to their respective tasks. Since the senator had budgeted only half an hour for the meeting, and had a committee meeting she had to get to, it was not long before Larry was back out in the front office. Larry had budgeted an hour, and his Uber driver was going to be meeting him out front at three on the dot, and besides, when he had first come in he had noticed with his keen-eyed backwoodsman glance that Jill was not exactly an eyesore. He had noticed that right off. She was not an eyesore, she had no ring on, she was tall, and he admired her apologetic methods. That was some fine way she had handled the protesters. There was also that.

It should not have been surprising. Jill was lively, intelligent, articulate, and quite lovely, but a disinterested observer might be forgiven if he wondered whether or not there might be insurmountable cultural differences between them. Jill was a native of Maryland, and she was broadly accustomed to the manners and customs of the western shore of the Chesapeake. Because of her upbringing, private education, and evangelical parents who had been wonderful to her, she very much approved of the kind of person that Larry Locke was, at least in theory, at least in the abstract. But she was about to be almost completely thrown off her game when she got to know him. An actual live one, one who was actually *like* that.

Given where she came from, it was not really possible to fault her for this, for she had acquired all of her principles from books. In fact, one of those books was *Ecochondriacs*, which she had read . . . and she had actually read it *twice*. It was currently in the back seat of her car, but she was really grateful that it wasn't here on her desk or anything. That way she wouldn't be tempted to ask for an autograph in the way that Eve had so naturally done. That would seem, I don't know, kind of *forward*. And speaking of being forward, she savagely rebuked herself for noticing that he didn't have a wedding band on. *Stupid* girl, she thought.

But the fact that she so thoroughly approved of the kind of man that Locke had seemed to be in print, and now even more in person, was more than a tad unsettling. It was an unsettled approval.

And so when the senator came out to head off to her committee meeting, and Larry came out at the same time, he showed no inclination to be leaving just yet. He walked over to Jill's desk slowly, and asked her a perfectly innocent question about whether the senator had produced any statement yet for her constituents on the pipeline bill that was likely going to be on the Senate floor this session. Jill said, no, no, not yet, probably next week. Larry said that he was interested in getting a copy, and she said okay.

From there the conversation moved seamlessly into other topics, and Eve's left eyebrow went up. Jill couldn't see Eve's eyebrow go up, but she could feel it going up. In the space of ten minutes they managed to touch on classical education, a mutual acquaintance in St. Louis, an appreciation for the Brandenburg Concertos, and Larry's almost total disinterest in how the Washington Nationals were going to do this season. That was the only source of potential conflict. Jill was an avid baseball fan, and was there at the stadium using up her season tickets as often as her schedule permitted. "It gives me an opportunity to yell at people without incurring any societal disapproval," she said. "That's an argument," Larry said.

This went on merrily until Larry pulled out his phone, glanced at it, and said, "Welp, gotta go. Don't want my Uber driver yelling at me. See you all around. Thanks for the hospitality."

And with that, he was gone, and he did it without bending any of the frames on the door.

When the door closed shut, and his form disappeared down the hallway to the right, Jill and Eve looked at each other for a moment.

"So then," Jill said, looking back down at her desk.

"You do know, " Eve said, "that *he* is going to be back. Within a few days, I should think. And he is going to ask you out. I think you should prepare yourself spiritually."

Jill waved her hand dismissively. "*Pppptt.* Whatever would make you think something like that?"

"Trevor took me hunting with him once. It was a beautiful hike into the back country that morning. We sat up on a small ridge over a broad meadow and shared a thermos of coffee. It was lovely, and *very* romantic, but I am getting off the point. After about an hour, at the very same moment, a sixteen-point buck came into the meadow from the right just as a beautiful doe came in from the left. I talked Trevor out of shooting the buck, which is why I think he doesn't take me out hunting any more."

"And your point . . .?"

"The picture was so beautifully framed. And I thought those two should have a chance to get better acquainted, as I am sure they did."

"That will be quite enough out of you," Jill said.

Eve laughed. "I don't think you could beat him up."

And that is why, later on in the evening, as Jill was preparing for bed, it occurred to her that she had talked to that protester woman that way because Larry was there, and she was showing off. She hissed at herself that she was being *so* junior high.

GINA SOFTENS, JUST A LITTLE

The following morning was not at all like anything Gina had ever experienced in her life, and it took all she had not to say anything about it in the moment.

When Del drove home the morning after his night at the hotel, he decided on the way home that he shouldn't say anything about what had happened to him, and especially about the voice. It was probably best since *he* didn't know what had happened to him, and Gina would probably think it was all some kind of manipulative trick anyhow. But he also knew that to say nothing at all would be the same as saying a great deal, and a great deal that was wrong, and so he resolved to gather up his work stuff before heading out to campaign headquarters, and speak briefly to Gina on the way out. And so that is exactly what he did.

She was in the kitchen, and so he stopped in on the way to the front door. "Gina," he said. "I know we can't talk about it now, and I don't know how to do this . . . but I do need to say one thing before I leave for headquarters . . . um . . . sorry for how I left last night . . . no, that's not right . . . I was *wrong* to leave last night, I was very wrong to be angry, and I completely understa . . . um . . . actually I probably don't understand, but I am trying . . . why you have decided to do what you obviously need to do. There. I am sorry. I will be back this evening by dinner, if that is all right with you. Will the boys be home?"

Gina turned around, and nodded briefly, both to acknowledge his comment and to indicate that the boys would be home. *Something is different*, she thought. *What is different?*

And she kept her own counsel for a full week following. Del was not on the road because of certain key Senate votes that were coming up, and so even though it was a busy time in the Senate, at least he was not off campaigning. And this meant that he was home every night for dinner, which is why Gina was quick to pick up on the fact that something was radically different. Their boys did, too.

About two days in, the oldest, twelve-year-old Will, asked his mother about it. "Mom, is something up with Dad?"

"Why do you ask, honey?" she said.

"Last night I asked him if he wanted to play chess, and he said *sure*. He just said sure. He never does that."

"Well, I do think something must be up, but I can honestly say that I have no idea what it might be." And these were true words. She had *no idea*.

Nobody had any idea, except for Del, and it was dawning on him, albeit somewhat *slowly*, that the Democratic nominee for the vice-presidency, a true-blue liberal and secular progressive, had prayed a prayer in a hotel room that was looking fair to turn him into a Jesus freak. This was not the sort of thing that turns up in a normal news cycle, and Del had a notion that when it did turn up there, it would appear in lurid and gaudy colors.

On the one-week anniversary of the day she had confronted him about Kara, she confronted him again about this new thing, whatever this new thing was. The boys were in bed and safely asleep—she had checked because they had the kind of house where voices carry—and she asked if he would be willing to talk for a few minutes. He said sure, and stuck his campaign briefing papers into his briefcase, and came out to the living room where she was, and sat down across from her.

"Okay," he said, spreading out his hands.

"All right, Del," she said. "I don't even know what I am asking for, or asking about. So the best thing I can come up with is 'what happened?'"

He grimaced slightly, drawing his breath in over his teeth. *This is it.* Stalling for a little bit of time, he said, "Why do you ask? What do you mean, 'what happened?'"

Gina sat for a moment. "Well, for the last week, you have been unbearably pleasant. Pleasant to be around. *Easy* to be around. Your apology last week was different from anything I have ever heard from you. And you have been so . . . pleasant . . . so easy . . . and all in the week after I caught you cheating on me *again*, and I honestly don't know what to make of it. None of this has changed my mind about the divorce or anything I said, but I will confess that my curiosity is kind of on fire."

Okay, Del thought. *Lord, help me out here. I don't know how to do this.*

"Okay," he said. "Promise to hear me out, and not to laugh at me?"

"Well, that's an odd request. But sure, I won't laugh."

And so Del explained the whole thing. He unloaded everything. He confessed to the two affairs that Gina had not known about. He told her that he had felt sexually entitled to whatever he had wanted since he first arrived in high school, and that he had decided at that time that it wasn't really anybody else's business. He said that she was completely in the right for wanting to divorce a man who was like that, and how his anger was an attempt to get her angry so he could justify things retroactively after the fact. "Please forgive me for that," he said. "I know I have done it many times. Too many to count, probably." And then he explained his sleeplessness at the hotel, how he got up, how he tried to watch some porn, and how he had stumbled onto the televangelist. And how he had gotten down on his knees and repented.

"The long and short of it, Gina," he said, "is that I think I got saved."

Gina sat quietly. Her reactions had been fluctuating wildly while he was talking. There was hope, then anger, then exasperation, then some more hope.

"Saved," she said. "Saved from *what*?"

"Well, principally from being the kind of toad I was being. But probably from Hell, too."

She flushed at the mention of Hell. Both Del and she had grown up in secular, liberated homes, and she felt like a fundamentalist just having the word mentioned in her living room. He noticed her discomfort, and said, "Look, I know next to nothing about all of this. I am only beginning to figure out what exactly has happened to me, and I am not expecting you to accept any of it. I am just trying to tell you what happened."

They both sat quietly for a couple of moments. Then he added, "Because I don't know anything, I ordered a couple of ebooks about religious experiences. That's where some of this language is coming from—getting saved, and all that."

"Has anybody in the Senate office noticed anything?" She asked. "Or at the campaign?"

"Well, Kara noticed," he said. "I broke up with her the next day. And a couple of staffers have mentioned in passing that I wasn't cussing them out like I usually do, and was anything wrong? But I have also been here a lot and not there."

"Maybe they won't notice," she said.

"No, they will," he said. "That is the thing about all this that is on my mind a great deal. The problem is that this . . . this event . . . didn't just affect my heart and my attitudes about adultery."

Gina looked up sharply at that. It was the first time in all their conflicts about his straying that he had ever used the word *adultery*.

"This has affected everything. It gets into everything, and I honestly don't know what I am going to do about it."

"I don't get it," she said.

"Well, you know that big climate change speech I am giving at the Smithsonian next week? I went over the draft today that the speech writers delivered to me. I have never read such a bowl of tripe in my life before. It is crammed full of lies, and half-truths, and then a layer of dishonest evasions. A month ago I would have asked for a bigger spoon and eaten the whole bowl. It turns out that Jesus has opinions on the ninth commandment, and not just the eighth."

Gina's eyebrows went up.

"Lying is the ninth," he said. "Adultery is the eighth. And I am not showing off. I had to look them up three times today."

Gina was still waiting, and for the last three minutes had been doing so on the angry side, and so Del continued. "What I am saying is that when it becomes obvious to my staff and to the DNC that I have turned into . . . into something else . . . they are going to have a major crisis on their hands. As will I." He almost said "as will we," but he caught himself just in time. Gina still noticed it. "I don't know what to do," he added. "*Nobody* to talk to about it."

Gina was thinking hard. *This is surreal.* She had known for years how ambitious he was, and how his eye had always been on the top slot, the presidency. *If he mentions stepping down from the nomination for veep, then I will know for sure that something is real about this.*

"I have been thinking about stepping down," he said.

TREVOR ENTERTAINS HIMSELF

Trevor and Eve were living in the D.C. area so he could get his MA in political science at the University of Maryland in College Park. The plan had been to start a family as soon as the Lord saw fit, but until that time arrived she was working for the senator and he was going to school. After that, he was thinking about law school because the law is "where a lot of the crazy is coming from."

When they had moved from Choctaw Valley, Trevor had settled into his studies easily, and found that his full-time load, given his energy levels, was really only about half time, and because his was a personality that was full of beans, with scarcely room left for even one more bean, he saw right away that he would have to find some edifying way to fill up the remainder of his time.

Inspired by some of the sting videos that O'Keefe and Daleiden had done, and also encouraged by the ongoing miniaturization of really high-quality camera and recording technology, Trevor had rigged up a high-tech baseball cap that would give him a quality recording of whoever he was talking to. And then, following an idea that had occurred to him in the shower, he had hit on the expedient of attending office hours for various professors at the university, whether he was enrolled in that class or not. If the class had over two hundred students, it was a pretty sure bet that the professor would have no idea that he wasn't in the class, and he could simply gather random footage of college professors saying outrageous things.

He had assumed, at the beginning of this noble enterprise, that over time he should be able to gather enough embarrassing footage to mug up a revelatory montage, and when he had three to five minutes' worth, he could then load it up onto YouTube in the hope that somebody would notice.

But if he had been an explorer, hunting for a lost city of gold, he was about to walk into the El Dorado of embarrassing statements. Had he been a prospector, hunting for gold, he was about to stumble on a nugget the size of a softball, lying in the middle of the path in front of him.

Having checked on his precious tri-tip, and having fooled around with his smoker some, he then turned to consider his schedule for the day. For the festivities of this particular afternoon, he had picked a mega-class taught by a Prof. Derek Laybourn, a man who was soon to become an Internet sensation.

When he got to the place in the spacious hallway indicated by the posted office hours, there was only one student ahead of him, and so he killed about fifteen minutes reading the cartoons on a neighboring professor's door, about a third of which were at least somewhat funny. The rest of them hammered away at various leftist talking points like they were the spike and the cartoons were a nine-pound sledge. *Ah well*, Trevor thought, turning away. The left can't meme, and the left can't tell jokes either.

The previous student, his questions answered or at least allayed, exited abruptly, and so Trevor took out his phone, opened the app that ran his camera and mic, and started recording. He then stepped into the doorway of the office, and tapped on the metal frame of the door tentatively. "Come in, come in," said a rotund and bombastic voice, sounding very much like someone named Derek Laybourn.

Trevor entered, somewhat slowly. His natural tendency was to bound into places, and, with Eve's encouragement, he had been trying to correct that deficiency. It tended to startle people. The course that he wasn't taking, but the office hours of which he was nevertheless showing up for, was called *Climate Change and the Revolution Now*. That had seemed promising. It had kind of jumped out at him when he was scrolling through the offerings.

Some people might think it dicey to go sit with a professor in his office hours in order to talk about a course you hadn't heard one word of, but Trevor had the kind of personality that was energized by living on the edge. But it was only living on the edge the first few times he had done it. After that, he had it all figured out, and this was one of those subsequent times. Professors liked to talk about themselves, and so the key was to ask them to talk about themselves. This was particularly the case with Derek Laybourn. His was an advanced case.

And so Trevor opened the proceedings up, with disingenuous charm, "Professor, I just have one question, and then I shall be out of your hair. Trying to integrate a lot of concepts here. I wanted to ask what is, *for you personally*, the central reason for treating climate change as seriously as you clearly do. I think it has something to do with how you named the course. I am thinking about that word *revolution*."

Laybourn swiveled in his chair, and reached for a shot glass of bourbon that he had put aside for the previous student. But confronted with a question about the *meta* like this, he decided he needed to resume his mid-afternoon second drink. The lubrication involved probably had something to do with the answer that kick-started Trevor into saying *ohboyohboyohboy* in the back recesses of his mind. But at the same time, Trevor's exterior remained placid and earnest.

"Thank you for not coming in here to ask me to count how many years the koala bears have left," Laybourn said. "And I can see from the way you phrased the question, that you have touched the central issue exactly."

Lucky, lucky, Trevor thought. But it was not really luck. Everything was connected if you just thought about it for a bit, and looked for the connections. Once you learn the discipline of worldview thinking, Trevor had concluded, other people think you are psychic.

"The climate change issues really are irrelevant. Climate change might be happening, might not be, we might be causing it, we might not be, it could be beneficial, it might be detrimental, who cares? *I* sure don't care. The polar bears can all go hang, for all I care. Some of the critics on the right are correct about *that* much, like that Locke pestilence. But what everybody seems to be missing, even some of the loyalists on our own side, is the relationship of cart and horse. It is not as though we are confronted with a natural disaster, and we on the left have come forward to offer the best of all available solutions to that disaster, that solution being our various proposals for climate change mitigation."

"Brilliant," Trevor said. "I suspected as much from something you said in your first lecture."

Trevor said this encouragingly, without any qualms at all, having worked through all the Ninth Commandment issues for his senior thesis back at Choctaw Valley Bible College. Dr. Tom had even been on his panel, and gave him the high praise of saying that he, Dr. Tom, would have to think about the issue some more. Trevor had taken the line that the Hebrew midwives were onto a good thing in lying to Pharaoh, that Rahab had done right by sending the pursuers galloping off in exactly the wrong direction, and that David was not offending against charity by pretending to be insane, much to the exasperation of Achish. The way Trevor saw it, Americans were not yet in a shooting war, but the cultural wars definitely were a time of war. It was a cold war, but a real one, and deception of the enemy was a legitimate tactic in war. Just think of Joshua at the second battle of Ai.

"Go on," he said. "This is why I came to talk to you. Glad I did. I normally never go to anybody's office hours."

"Well, a quick study like you shouldn't need to," Laybourn said. He was very conceited to begin with, and also very smart, which needed to be shown off, and the bourbon had kicked in, deciding to do all in its power to help Trevor out. Unbeknownst to Laybourn, it was a Christian bourbon, named after the eighteenth-century Baptist minister Elijah Craig. And it was a *premium* Christian bourbon, all in all, making it a good afternoon for Trevor.

"The crying need for revolution is the real disaster. *That* crisis has hundreds of symptoms, of which climate change could be one. I don't care. If climate change turns out to be a big nothing, as some of the data suggest it might, I for one am willing to drop it like a hot rock. We can replace it instantly. It will be replaced by ten other crises, each of which will make the same point, that point being the absolute necessity of revolution. We haven't had the revolution yet. *That*'s the crisis. That is the thing that will kill all of us. We do not reason from climate change to the revolution, but rather from the revolution to any cause that will help us toward that deliverance. And climate change will certainly do, but in the long run it is irrelevant. Climate change doesn't really matter, and burning all the churches does. And if the churches burn, I don't care about the carbon footprint."

Laybourn's eyes had gotten heated, not with anger, but with passion. He looked just like an end times speaker that had come to the Bible college campus once time during Trevor's freshman year. Trevor had been in the front row, and had gotten a glimpse of that kind of fevered thinking close up and personal. *No, thank you very much*, had been his reaction.

Their visit went on for ten more minutes, with each minute getting riper and juicier than the previous one. Trevor was acutely aware of the fact that the pauses in the conversation were starting to get a little longer, and so, lest he wear out his welcome, he abruptly stood up.

"Well," he said, "you have answered my question in full, and with something extra. You've given me a lot to think about it. I thank you, good sir."

Trevor stopped at the bottom of the large staircase that went down to the main entrance in order to pull out his phone. He wanted to ensure that everything recorded properly. It had.

Trevor then tugged on the brim of his cap and smiled. He was going to go home to Eve right quick, and display some of his male plumage. This being his lucky day, perhaps the evening would progress to the point of conceiving their first child.

But at almost the same instant, Trevor caught his reflection in a glass doorway across the hallway, and a little wave in the glass made his head look like a balloon. He suddenly laughed at himself. *No, better not. Not like that*, he thought. *Don't want a kid with a dad like that.*

CODY GETS SOME NEWS

After he and Helen had teamed up in their on-the-run *ad hoc* arrangement, Cody had managed to take some personal leave. He had accumulated quite a number of vacation days, and when it came to teaching his classes, he was between terms. That was settled easily enough via email. A few of his friends in Lynchburg had wondered casually if he had fallen off the earth, but he was able to put them off without actually lying about anything. You can lie in a war, but not to your friends. Even so, appealing to "personal time" was much more duddy than saying he was on the lam with a beautiful atheist. But he could tell everybody about that later, he hoped.

He was flipping through his emails on his phone while Helen went into a CVC to get a few personal items, and he was nearing the end of the stack of emails when she opened the door and hopped back in the car.

"Go ahead and finish," she said. "We are just driving in circles anyway. And we are not in any real hurry to get back *here*."

Cody got to his last email, read the subject line, suddenly started, and sat up straight. "Oh my," he said, before catching himself.

"What?" Helen asked.

He started to answer her, and then stopped. He hurriedly opened the email and scanned the first paragraph, grinning widely. He wasn't sure how he was going to explain it to her. His article on a second-century fragment of the book of Ephesians had cleared the hurdle of peer review and had been accepted by one of the more prestigious journals of textual criticism. That fragment covered a chapter and a half of the epistle, and Cody had sought to demonstrate that the original of this manuscript necessarily belonged to the Byzantine text type, as opposed to the Alexandrian. The fact that the editors of the journal were strong advocates of the anything-but-Byzantine text type meant either that they were feeling unusually charitable, or that the peer reviews came back unusually strong. Or maybe the editors were just trying to demonstrate their even-handedness so they could justify lambasting him and his argument in a future issue.

So Cody explained the outline of his article, sort of, and Helen thought she understood most of his explanation, sort of. At least she understood peer review, and the importance of publishing. "Well, that is good news," she said. "Congratulations."

The news of this acceptance had also been cc'd to Cody's department head, who had been a thorn in Cody's side ever since he had arrived at Liberty. It was pressure from him, actually, one Dr. Jerry Sommerville, that had made Cody get serious about writing for publication in the first place. But the congratulatory note that was sent from the journal included at the bottom the abstract of the article Cody had submitted, and this is how it happened that Sommerville took an interest in it for the first time, having read something about it for the first time.

And this is why, about fifteen minutes later, Cody's phone chirruped a new notification at him. It was Sommerville, saying that it was essential that Cody come down from Annapolis at once. They needed to talk. Like, right now.

"Well," Cody said, turning to Helen. "It is not that far to drive. I don't think anybody knows for sure that you are with me, and we might as well drive in a straight line as drive in circles in the Washington/Baltimore metroplex. Nobody's looking for my car, at least that we know of, and I can get the back windshield fixed in Lynchburg. I can talk to Sommerville, allay any concerns he might have, and that will signal to anybody who inquires that my life is still doing its ordinary, somewhat boring, thing."

"Allay any concerns he might have?" Helen said. "What possible concerns could someone have over an article about an ancient manuscript?"

"Well," Cody said, "the people who are after you are not trying to kill you because you have a disagreement over how much sunshine all of us are getting. They are coming after you because of *money*. They have a racket going, and you have some information that threatens that racket."

"Well, sure. True enough," she said. "But how does that apply to this?"

"I don't know that it does," Cody replied. "But it *could*. In fact, I have been praying that it would."

Helen didn't roll her eyes when he mentioned his prayers, but if we are being frank with ourselves we have to acknowledge that she did think about it. But she was still interested, in spite of herself.

"Yes. But *how* could it?"

"Well, you see, over a hundred million Bibles are printed annually. It is really big business. Most of them are copyrighted translations, and they are translated from a particular manuscript family. If anybody important paid any attention to my article, if it caught fire in any way, a lot of people could be really unhappy. And they will be unhappy to the tune of hundreds of millions of dollars. But there are lots of *ifs* in there."

"But obvious enough that your boss wants to have a heart-to-heart with you?"

"Yeah," Cody said. "Looks like it." And he took a moment to write Sommerville back to say that he could be down there the next day, and would two p.m. work? "Yes, it would," the reply came back a moment later.

* * *

The next day, Cody walked into Jerry Sommerville's office confidently enough, at two p.m. on the dot, but he was inwardly tentative. He didn't really know what Sommerville was going to say or do.

"Hi, Jerry," he said when he came in.

Jerry grunted. He was the kind of gruff character who *would* grunt, even if he were delighted. He looked like a scholar, or perhaps like a mad scientist. His white hair stuck out from behind his ears, and his goatee was closer to gray than white. The grunt sounded like something in the neighborhood of "sit down," and so Cody shut the door, and sat down.

Sommerville didn't mess around. He got straight to the point. He didn't put any varnish on his words at all. He had apparently been stewing about it all night. And as one of the senior editors of the soon-to-be-released *Discipleship Study Bible*, he had gone through several very awkward conversations with his publisher the night before. They had gotten wind of the article around the same time that Sommerville had, probably from one of the scholars who had been on the peer review board.

"Cody, you have to pull that article. You need to ask them not to publish it. You need to say that certain critical information has just come to your attention."

"But it hasn't," Cody said. "No critical information has come to my attention."

"I was referring to the fact that if that article runs, you are out of a job. I would say that was critical information."

Cody rocked back in his chair. He wasn't expecting anything like this. "I don't understand," he said finally.

"What's not to understand? Pull the article or get fired. We can't have a member of our department publishing an article like that on the eve of the release of the *Discipleship Study Bible*. I am telling you straight up, not going to lie. Of course if you repeat any of this, I will deny it in cold blood, also straight up. In that case, you were fired for insubordination and a few other items in your personnel file that I would rather not go into."

"But . . . what about academic freedom? . . . what about my arguments? . . . what about the *truth*?"

"What did you get your doctorate in? Idealism? On hobbits dancing in meadows?"

Cody sat still for a moment, still stunned. Sommerville started up again, not unkindly. "I don't know how much lead time it would take for you to get the article canceled. But if you were just notified about the acceptance yesterday, I am sure I can give you a day to think about it. But at the end of that day of thinking about it, I need that article deep-sixed."

Cody looked up at him. "Oh, I don't need any time to think about it. The article stays right where it is. And the arguments need to be *answered*. And you wouldn't need to fire me. I can have a letter to you by tomorrow morning. Whichever you prefer."

Sommerville sat for a moment, surprised himself at the turn things had taken. After scratching his goatee for a minute, he said, again not unkindly, "I'll take the letter."

With that, Cody stood up, half-saluted Sommerville, and headed out. He had left Helen with the car at the Windshield Doctor that was just a few blocks off campus. He would walk back out to the shop, gather everything up, and they could hit the road again. He found himself smiling to himself as he imagined himself telling Helen about it. "It seems we *both* have trouble with bosses."

An hour later, they were back in the car, heading north on 301. They had grabbed some fast food, and were eating as they drove. They had decided some time before that they would have to put everything on Cody's card, and not Helen's, because if at some point they found themselves tracked by pros, as it looked like they might be, the bad guys would probably have ways to track any activity that had anything to do with Helen's accounts. So her accounts had been entirely inactive the last few days, as silent as a really silent grave. But as they pulled out of Burger King this time, Helen felt she had to say something again. "Remember that I will pay you back, at least fifty/fifty, when this is all over. Promise."

"That was our deal," Cody had said, "although I am not worried about it."

"Well, thanks," she said. "But I *want* you to be worried about it."

"A guy in my position doesn't get many opportunities to date an evolutionary atheist, and so the least I could do is pick up the tab." He realized, as soon as the words were out of his mouth, that he was flirting. *Stupid, stupid, stupid. Reel it in, Cody.*

"These aren't dates," she said. "We are on the run from killers, or I am at least, and you are a very nice man who is helping me. That is not what I call a date."

"I know," he said. "They can't be considered dates technically. But I can pretend, can't I?" *Stupid man! Flirting with an atheist?* Cody suddenly realized that his internal moral monitor, his robust conscience, was going to wake up any minute and start swearing at him like a machinist mate on a tramp steamer. That would not be good. *That* would be unsettling. Evangelical consciences usually don't cuss like that.

Cody promptly decided he needed to change the subject, and then that would keep him from flirting with her anymore. So he trotted out his observation about the trouble they were both having with their bosses. It was the wrong move.

"You really think that getting fired is equivalent to a hit man showing up at your place at dawn in order to shoot you? You really *think* that?" She had understood at least the beginnings of a flirtation and decided she needed to restore some distance. He was cute and everything, but he was still a Jesus freak, and he wrote articles about which piece of paper came from where two thousand years ago.

"Well, of course not . . ." he began. He was going to continue with his explanation of his lame attempt at humor when the back windshield, newly installed just that afternoon, exploded. Someone had shot at them again. This time it was on the driver's side.

CHAPTER 5

Striking Out

HELEN BLOWS UP

Helen spun around in her seat, and got up on her knees, peering over the back of her seat. There was only one nondescript car behind them, and it was slowing down to take an exit they were just passing.

"They blew out your back window, and just left!"

Cody continued to drive on, staring at the road, thinking hard.

Helen was staring at him. "What are you going to do?"

"I haven't an earthly," he said. "Find another windshield repair place probably. We have another two hours to Annapolis, which leaves us plenty of time."

The car was silent for a moment, except for the sound of rushing wind past the back window. Cody's phone suddenly chirruped loudly. He pulled it out of his jacket pocket, and handed it to Helen. "What's it say?"

She fumbled for a few moments, trying to get to his texts, but when she got there, she looked up in amazement. "It just says, 'Pull the article.' That blast was a warning for *you*."

Cody was scratching his chin, muttering to himself. What he was muttering was "not Sommerville." He had always considered his boss to be an irascible and unreasonable human being, but he did think of him as a human being. And he also thought of him as a convinced Christian of some order. "Not Sommerville," he said again.

Helen was glaring at him. Finally she said, "How do *you* rate?"

Cody looked over in surprise. "What?" he said.

"I said, 'How do you rate?'"

"What do you mean?" He was genuinely startled.

"I mean that threatening you by blowing out your windshield is the lamest thing ever. Over what? Over how many *thees* and *thous* were in the original book of Ephesians?"

Cody shook his head, and started to take the bait. "Well, that is a gross simplification of what my article was saying, in the first place . . ."

Helen interrupted him. "And simplified or not, what would it matter?"

Cody's eyes widened some more, and they had already been wide. "Why, you're *jealous*," he said.

"Am not," she retorted. "Ridiculous. What would I be jealous of?"

Cody laughed out loud. Everything came into focus. "You're jealous because you were the one that somebody was trying to kill, and now I have caught up with you. Now somebody has threatened to kill me, and this has radically leveled the playing field. The score is now tied."

Helen swore at him, and he laughed again, which made her angrier.

"Getting shot at is not some kind of *contest*, you dope. What kind of sense would that make?"

"It makes no sense at all," he replied. "It *shouldn't* be a contest. So why are you jealous? I was not arguing that it made any kind of sense. I was just saying that you were jealous."

Helen sputtered for a moment, and then said, "I'm not talking to you anymore. Makes no sense to talk with you if you are going to be like that."

And so they drove in silence for the next forty-five minutes. Helen was furious for the first ten minutes or so of that forty-five, and then in a state of absolute emotional churn for the thirty minutes after that. She had grown up with three younger brothers who all adored her, and she had a doting father on top of that. And so she had figured out, very early on in her life, that outbursts of temper were the best way to steer things in directions more to her liking. Her mother saw what she was doing, but really didn't have the wherewithal to stop it. Her father and brothers didn't have *any* idea of what was going on. And no one in the family had connected their indulgence of her fits and tempers with the fact that she had walked away from the faith, not to mention the Fremont Bible Chapel, in her first year away at college. She had told herself that it was the rigors of scientific inquiry that did her faith in, but it was actually the fact that she was looking for a wider scope for her passions and piques. She thought her loss of faith was intellectual, but it was almost entirely emotional.

Cody just drove on in silence, eyes on the road. He didn't seem angry or upset at her at all. He was just driving along, eyes on the road.

When her churn started to subside, she finally—after some hesitation—broke the silence. "No need to fight," she said.

"I agree," he replied. "No need."

"I am sorry for my outburst," she said after another moment.

"Apology accepted, and thank you," he said.

Another mile marker flashed by.

"Aren't you going to say *you're* sorry?" She asked. This is what had always happened with her brothers. When her behavior had been so egregious that she knew that an apology was needed, she would offer it, and then level things up again afterwards by getting her brothers to apologize also. And they always did. The male Greenes were a species that valued keeping the peace in the household very highly.

Cody, on the other hand, had only done that one time in his life. He had been ten years old, and had gotten into a skirmish with one of the neighbor boys. It was the other kid's fault entirely, but afterward, the boy had provoked Cody into apologizing also, as a way of settling their peace treaty. Cody's brother had been a witness to the whole debacle, and when the story came out that night at the dinner table, Cody—to his great astonishment at the time—found himself taken down to the basement and switched. For lying to the neighbor kid.

After the whole thing was over, his father, a gruff concrete worker who went by Hank, took him by both shoulders, looked him straight in the eye and said, "Son, I don't want you to ever apologize to somebody just because *they* say to. If you owe them one, don't make them ask. You should be there ahead of them. And if you don't owe them one, then your apology is not anything with them. It is trying to put things back together on the foundation of a lie. And lies always collapse under any weight you try to put on them."

Cody had never forgotten that, and it had become one of the guiding principles of his life. He didn't know it, but it was the reason why he had refused to pull his article. The roots from that tree his father had planted for him were all over his front yard.

And this is why, when Helen asked him if he was going to apologize to her, he shook his head *no*. "No," he said. "I don't think I wronged you in any way. I would be happy to consider whether I did though. I will think and pray about it."

Helen turned away with a little exclamation, and stared out the window for a time. She felt something going on inside her that mystified and scared her. She was appalled by, and powerfully attracted to, *something*.

ROCCO AGAIN

Rocco had connections. He had plants. He had moles. This meant that he had a reliable flow of information coming to him at all times. And he had an organizing kind of mind and an uncanny ability to keep track of many different threads at once. One of his leisure activities was the reading of detective fiction, and then writing up critiques of the discovered culprit afterwards. His mind was really good at finding patterns and assembling clues.

The people who sent all this information to Rocco did not know that they were serving as the *ad hoc* intelligence agency for a hit man. They just knew that if they shared information with him, apparently harmless information, then a very nice sum of money would appear in their checking account within two business days. They knew they were breaking the rules of whatever establishment employed them, but they didn't need to inquire about the uses to which the information was put. It most certainly would not be put to nefarious purposes. They were counting on that. Man was basically good, right?

This was an arrangement that Rocco had with more than a handful of individuals at the NSA, the CIA, the IRS, the FBI, numerous metropolitan police departments up and down the east coast, along with state DMVs. Their soft corruption was put to hard uses by him, but nobody expected *them* to know that.

Hugh was on his list of individuals needing a visitation, but not at the top of it. Maurice and Leon had been different—they had been directly involved in the attempted hit, and could easily spill something valuable to the cops. So once they were out of the way, Rocco's attention turned to the task of finding Helen. Hugh could wait a bit.

Rocco decided to start with the neighbors, and identifying who had driven Helen away. But rather than doing a little sleuthing of his own, he decided to tap a resource that he had on retainer in the Annapolis Police Department. The name of the person who drove off with Helen Greene that morning? He had the answer in fifteen minutes. Cody Vance. From there he was able to get the license plate number, and from there he had someone who could do a search of all the traffic surveillance cameras in the area, and to give him a map of where Cody and Helen had been. They had apparently been driving around in circles mostly, and with one jaunt down to Lynchburg. They were apparently still down there.

Presumably they were going to be coming back up. They didn't appear to have any particular plan. So Rocco had men placed at all the on ramps on the northwards side of the toll booths on the main routes north. He had his source with the state police send him a notice pronto when those plates came through the staked toll, and then he could have his man on the scene get on the tollway and drive real slow until he was passed by a black Tahoe. It worked like a charm, and he had a firm tail on Cody and Helen almost right away. Rocco sent out word to his other men on stand by that they were dismissed for the evening, and then sent word to Oscar and Dante that their services would likely be required later on that night.

The man tailing Cody and Helen, whose name was Joaquin, called Rocco up about a half an hour after he made contact. "Real curious thing, boss," he said. "I was following 'em, standard distance, when this pick-up blows by me, and shoots out their back windshield, and then exits, smooth as hot butter. Probably fake plates, but I got a picture of 'em for ya. Somebody else is in this game."

"Huh," Rocco said. "Let me think about that one. Wouldn't be the first time."

Rocco had Cody's credit card numbers, and he also had somebody who could tell him if anybody had used one of them to purchase something, or make a reservation. That answer came back promptly also. *Holiday Inn Express* in Culpeper. The people he had on retainer liked his meaty approach to bonuses, and that is why he consistently got good results. All those overhead costs were going to be passed along to Steven Lee anyhow.

Culpeper would be perfect. Oscar and Dante weren't that far away and could get there well before Cody and Helen.

He put his phone down, and starting rubbing his forehead. Who else could be after Helen? He decided to give Steven Lee a call, and give him a little unshirted hell. That might shake something loose.

To think was to act. He probably ought to have called Lee by this point anyhow. He was not wrong—Steven Lee jumped at the call. "Any news?" he said querulously. It sounded like someone was messing with his tremolo knob.

Rocco explained, in his smoothest professional manner, that he had the needed info on them, and that now it was just a matter of time. No worries, all was well in hand. Well in hand. Don't worry about it. Stop worrying about it.

He then moved smoothly into the purpose of his call, which was to put Steven Lee even further back on his heels, and shake loose any useful information that might fall off him. "So what did you mean by hiring another outfit to deliver the hit? Didn't you know that that is the way for someone to get badly hurt?" Rocco pulled out his very best, raspy, accusative voice.

The implication was not lost on Lee, and so he quavered a little bit more than previously. "What do you mean? I *didn't* hire anybody else. Only you. I mean, I hired that Hugh guy, but that was before I called you. That's it, honest."

The quavering had the ring of sincerity, the tremolo levels of truth. Rocco spoke a little more softly. "Well, my man was tailing your two lovebirds earlier today on the freeway, and someone in a pick-up truck drove right by him, as sleek as dammit, and blew out their back windshield."

As it happened, Steven Lee was an aficionado of action movies, and he saw an immediate problem. Despite his nervousness in talking to Rocco, he couldn't help himself. This was an area where he had some real expertise. He had even submitted some film reviews to different blog sites under a pseudonym, and two of them had actually been published. "That's not an attempted hit, is it? That was a *warning*. I don't think you should be asking who else is trying to bump them off besides you. You should be asking what the warning is for. I need Helen out of the picture because of something she already did. But a warning is over something that might happen in the future. That's not Helen. That's your other guy, that's Cody. I don't know what he might do, but it must be pretty ripe."

Rocco gruffly ended the call, set his phone down, and stared at it malevolently. He was clearly losing a step or two. He swore at himself savagely. *Lee* of all people.

HELEN SWINGS AND MISSES

In their travels together, both Helen and Cody had picked up a medium-sized roller suitcase each, and had purchased, all on

Cody's credit card, enough clothes and toiletries to get them through. "To get us through whatever it is we think we are doing," Helen had said.

And so it was, at the hard end of the day, around ten thirty p.m., they found themselves standing outside their hotel rooms, number 106 and number 108 respectively, fumbling with their keys. The hotel was not exactly crawling with guests, and the parking lot was nearly empty. They felt entirely alone. The desk clerk had actually cocked an eyebrow when they got two rooms, as much as to tell Cody that if *he* were traveling around with someone who looked like that, they wouldn't be getting no two rooms.

And Helen had apparently been thinking along the same lines, despite the tiff they had had earlier in the day. Or perhaps *because* of the tiff. Right after her door didn't open for the second time, she gave a little exclamation of frustration, and then, before he got his door open, she stepped across quickly and kissed Cody full on the mouth, as warm and as seductive as she knew how to make it.

He kissed her back for about a second and a half, and then jumped the same way he had once jumped when a waiter had dropped a hot bowl of French onion soup in his lap. "Whoa," he said. *Whoa, whoa, whoa.* "Yikes," he added.

She stood there in mock belligerence, in flirty fight mode. "What?" she said. "I asked you a question. You gonna answer me?"

"Um," he said, trying to gather up his thoughts, which someone had grabbed and then kicked all over the parking lot. It was probably the devil, and he was doing a lot of kicking.

"I . . . I do owe you an answer," he said. "And we obviously need to talk. Probably should have talked way before this. Look.

We are both grown-ups and, um, given these, um, overtures, we obviously need to speak frankly."

"Okay, then," she said. "Speak frankly then. But it wasn't an overture. It was a kiss."

"All right, let's start with this. I *am* willing to speak with you frankly, but not within fifty yards of a bed. That's the first frank thing. You drop your stuff off inside, and I'll do the same, and let's meet back out here in sixty seconds and go for a walk."

At the far end of the parking lot a black sedan was parked, tucked away deep in shadows of the corner. Behind the wheel were a couple of Rocco's operatives, his explosives guys. Their car looked like it had been parked there for a couple weeks, having that deserted feel. But it wasn't deserted at all, and Oscar and Dante just sat there watching as Cody and Helen went into their rooms. Oscar offered Dante a cinnamon-flavored toothpick, and started the engine up.

"Perfect," Oscar said. They pulled around to the other side of the motel, got out, and opened the trunk of the car, and began working over a duffle bag that was in there, looking for all the world like a couple of travelers messing around with their luggage.

In the meantime, back on the other side of the motel, Cody and Helen came out of their rooms, walked down the sidewalk to the main thoroughfare, turned right, and headed down toward a Denny's that was located within a block or so. About five minutes after they had disappeared, Oscar and Dante came around the corner, handling the duffle bag like a couple of pros, which they were. The parking lot was still deserted, except for

Cody's car, which was still there, and the lights in both rooms were out. The two had clearly gone to bed.

Meanwhile Cody and Helen had both received their drinks, and Cody, who had been thinking furiously this entire time, said, "Look . . ." He stopped because they both heard a muffled *whommpppff* in the distance, like a distant jet breaking the sound barrier. But nothing followed, and so Cody resumed.

"Look," he said again. "We are still speaking frankly, right? I am *very* attracted to you, which you no doubt picked up on, and apparently it is reciprocal. Sorry for flirting with you earlier, by the way. That was way out of line—joking about us dating. So on one level, I would like nothing more than to make love to you. Simple honesty. But there is this other level, and it involves the entirety of my life. I am a Christian, and what we might want to call a romp, God's law forbids as fornication."

"Well, look at it from *my* point of view," she said. "I had to get over the idea of sex with a Jesus freak myself. We all have to make our little sacrifices."

Cody laughed. "Right. But from your vantage, these things seem to be like individual quirks or hang ups, entirely personal. For me, apart from not being able to live with my conscience, and not being able to pursue a more serious relationship with you, because a Christian can't marry a non-Christian . . ."

"*Marry?*" Helen exploded. "Who's talking about marriage? I didn't propose, and I certainly didn't expect *you* to."

Cody was pushing his coffee cup back and forth. "It is a basic part of Christian ethics that sex is reserved for marriage."

Helen just stared at him, still glaring but with no little affection mixed in with it. "Well, I do have to say that this is the weirdest brush-off *I* have ever gotten."

Cody smiled, somewhat grimly. "If it is any consolation, this has everything to do with my relationship with Christ, and nothing to do with whether or not I think we would have a lot of fun. We *would*, and then I would be a total wreck tomorrow. You would probably have to drive."

"Well, okay. Suit yourself, Galahad. I still think you are making mountains out of molehills."

"Not exactly. If we did this, and then I tried to tell you something about Jesus tomorrow, who would turn on me with her rapier wit and say, 'You weren't thinking about Jesus very much last *night* though'? And you would be dead right, and I would have no answer."

"Okay," Helen said, nodding. "Fair point. I would say something like that, and I can understand why you wouldn't want something like that to happen."

The atmosphere warmed up considerably after that, they talked some more, for about half an hour more, and then they both stood up to head back to the motel. As soon as they got up from their booth, Cody leaned over and kissed her on the forehead. "Thanks much," he said.

"You're welcome," she said, grateful for the gesture, and yet not sure what he was thanking her for.

They walked slowly back to the motel, but before they turned into the parking lot they noticed an eerie glow extending out into the street. When they turned into the parking lot, they both stopped, flummoxed. The parking lot was jammed with fire engines, and the wing of the motel where their rooms had been was ablaze. Flames were shooting up twenty feet past the roofline, which was already showing signs of collapsing. They could feel the heat from where they stood.

Cody's car was on fire also, the front end twisted beyond all description. Helen started to walk toward the nearest fire engine, but Cody grabbed her by the arm.

"We have to talk to somebody," she said.

"No, no, we really don't. Not unless you want to be scooped right up into police custody, and have your story told on all the news sites. It seems to me that the one thing we do not want is for *anybody* to know where you got to, or who you are with right now."

Helen nodded, slowly. "Right. You're right. So what are we going to do?"

Cody took a deep breath. "First, let's head back to Denny's before someone notices us and asks us any questions. You have your purse? The thumb drive and your gun? Good. And I have my wallet and credit cards. Why don't we go back to the restaurant and call a cab from there? We can have him drive us out to the airport, which isn't far from here, and we can rent a car there."

"Well, absent anything better to do, let's try it."

CHAPTER 6

Oppo Research

CLOSE QUARTERS

As they had been spending more and more hours on the run, both Cody and Helen had begun to grow extremely wary, and cagey. They started to park the car a few streets over from any restaurant they decided to visit so as not to have the car possibly spotted by someone, and them sitting inside, thirty seconds away, as vulnerable as you please. And it had also occurred to them that credit card use could probably be tracked, even if they didn't know yet that it was Cody who had spirited Helen away. So he had hit one ATM downtown, and gotten a couple thousand dollars out of savings. They were then able to pay cash for all their meals and other incidentals.

The evening after they had gotten back from Lynchburg, they had spotted a restaurant they thought looked unobtrusive, and they went and parked the rental three or four blocks away. "And the walking should do us some good," Cody said, "after driving around all day."

But after they had walked for a block, and much to their surprise, they came on an abandoned school building, one that had the look of a junior high about it. "Early seventies," Cody said. "I went to one just like that." There was a huge parking lot in the middle, with knee-high weeds growing up through the aged asphalt, weeded ball fields off to the left, only identifiable through a sagging chain link backstop, and off to the right was the school. It still looked entirely serviceable, but Cody guessed that an ambitious superintendent had gotten a bond levy passed, and was now tormenting his prisoners at a swankier location.

They got to the restaurant and ordered their meals, and were each silently critical of the other's dietary choices. Cody had ordered chicken-fried steak, and Helen had ordered a kale salad. Their meal passed in small talk, but when Helen was finishing her salad, she couldn't resist one comment. "That salad was really good. I am surprised that a place that could make a salad that good would even *have* something like chicken fried steak, as you call it, on the menu." As she was talking she noticed that there was a little extra dig in her comment that she tried to fix at the end of the sentence with a little lilt in her laugh.

And Cody didn't seem to notice anything wrong, because he laughed too, and said, "Well, *yeah*. And I was surprised that a place that would serve kale salad would know how to make chicken fried steak. But they sure did." Helen's jab, which she had decided halfway through shouldn't have been a jab, had gone whistling over his head. He wasn't embarrassed about anything at all. *How could you be embarrassed about eating a chicken fried steak?*

As they were walking back to the car, and were crossing the school grounds again, for some reason Cody felt an odd sensation running up his neck, and he turned around and looked back the way they had come. The back parking lot of the restaurant abutted the property of the old school, and was about the length of a football field away. Two men were climbing out of a car that was facing them. One of them jerked, and pointed at them, and the other one walked around to the front of the car and stepped through the hole in the fence that Cody and Helen had just come through. The other man followed him.

They hadn't been tailed, Cody was sure of it. This was sheer bad luck. And they had limited choices. If they ran for it, they would probably not make it. There was no place to hide off to their right where the ball fields were. That left the school, which was only twenty yards off to their left. If they ran, it would confirm their identity, but when Cody glanced back again, he saw the two men were already running.

"Come on," he said, and bolted for the concrete steps that ran up to the front doors. Please, please, don't be locked, Cody thought. But when they got there he realized the question was immaterial. The window to the right of the main doors had been broken out, and replaced, like ages ago, with a piece of plywood. That piece of plywood had been knocked askew by others who wanted access to the school for some reason, and all Cody had to do was push on it slightly to make a hole large enough for them to step through, first Helen, and then Cody.

There was a fairly large atrium with a bank of what had been the school offices off to the right, and a broad stairway along the left wall. Straight ahead was a passageway that looked as though it emptied into a gym. They stood momentarily. "Our strategy right now is hiding, not fighting," Cody said. "Where would the best opportunities for hiding be?"

"Upstairs," they both said at the same moment.

A second later, Cody and Helen were running up the stairs together, with Cody slowing down a few times to wait for her. At the first landing, he extended his hand and she took it, and they dashed up the second flight together. Both of them were panting at the top, and instinctively they both turned down the hallway that went to the right.

It was an old school building, and so they ran past five or six classrooms. At the end of the hall, everything opened out into a broad and well-lit room, one that looked like it had once been used for band practice or something like that. On the far side of the room was a set of double doors, and another set of stairs that went back down to the first floor.

"They will totally expect us to run down there, trying to get to ground level again," Cody said, still panting.

"Don't we *want* to get to ground level again?" Helen asked.

"Sure thing. After they are long gone." Cody took a few steps back down the hallway, past the girls' restroom, and pushed on the next door and peered inside. "*Hurry!*" Helen said behind him.

It was a storeroom, crammed with old desks, blackboards on rolling wheels, audio visual carts, and many other articles that spoke solemnly of the fact that education did indeed cast off detritus. Cody looked down at the floor and along the wall on the right side saw a place he thought they could manage to crawl through.

Along the back wall, he could see a row of rolled up carpets, standing on end, like a line of stiff soldiers.

He turned to Helen, and pointed to the crawl space. "Give me the gun," he said. "I will come right after you."

He would not have attempted it had not some enterprising soul unrolled one of the carpets and put it on the floor before stashing all the equipment in there. If the floor had been simply tile, Cody was sure their crawl tracks would have been visible in the dust, and that would have been far too great a risk.

Helen had given him the gun, seeming kind of glad about it, and promptly disappeared. Cody heard one of the two men downstairs kicking the plywood in, and he shut the door of the storeroom partially, got on his hands and knees and followed Helen to the back wall. When he was about four feet in, he hooked his left leg on a desk behind him, and pulled it into their passageway.

When he got to the back of the storeroom, he found Helen standing in the corner where the crawl space ended. He stood up beside her, gingerly, and found that there was scarcely room for the two of them. He turned around cautiously and saw that their heads were both sticking up above the furniture. It was either kneeling down, or getting behind the line of rolled-up carpets. If the bad guys came in to look for them in here, he would much rather be standing up. And behind the carpets he would be in a position to use the gun.

In the distance he heard voices, he thought coming up the main stairs. He put the gun in his belt, and pushed and pulled at the nearest two carpet rolls. With a good deal of effort, he cleared a space where the two of them could stand.

"I will go in first," he said, "and have my back to the wall. I want to be able to use the gun if I have to, and will need a clear line of sight." He had that in a two-inch slit between the two carpet rolls he had moved. "Then you come in."

He scooted around Helen, got his back to the wall, and slid sideways into the space he had made. When he was settled, he reached out his left hand, and drew her in. She was facing him, back to the door, and was leaning heavily on his chest. He got the gun out of the belt, and held it up at the ready.

All the two of them could hear at first was the sound of their own breathing, along with a couple of heartbeats badly out of sync, both of which they thought were making an enormous racket. After their breathing subsided, they could only hear their hearts beating, but not quite as raucous, and then, voices in the hall way outside.

"They could have gone into any of these classrooms," one of the voices said.

"Why would they do that?" the second man said. "They's trying to get away."

"What would you do?" The first voice asked, pushing the storeroom door open with the barrel of a pistol.

"Me? I'm a high-tailer, not a hider . . . damn!"

"What?" The first voice said.

"A staircase, over there, running straight back down to God's green grass. C'mon." Cody heard footsteps running.

"You sure? . . . oh, never mind."

But Cody and Helen stood right where they were until the sun went down. Cody's right leg went completely to sleep, and he started to wonder if he would even be able to crawl out when they finally decided to try. Or if he would do so dragging one leg behind him.

Helen went first, and got out easily. Cody made heavy weather of it. He decided his leg wasn't actually asleep, but rather in some sort of a coma. When he finally made it to the end of their little crawl tunnel, he tried to stand up, and the only reason he didn't go completely over was that he hit the wall with his left shoulder. "Mercy," he said. "We will have to stand here for a bit until my leg joins us again. Unless you want to carry me back to the car."

Helen laughed at that, and when she was done, the old school returned to complete silence. Cody noticed that Helen didn't ask for her gun back.

THE SET UP

Billy Jerome was a typical politician who looked like a statesman. He had white hair that was thick and full, and which reached almost to his shoulders. He looked like a cross between an aging hippie running a tie dye shop and a Confederate general. His jaw was square and solid, making it look like he had a lot more character going on inside than he actually did. That jaw had actually a great deal to do with his success in politics up to this point, which was considerable.

For Billy Jerome was Bryan McFetridge's running mate. He had been picked because he had won a hard-fought Senate race in Pennsylvania, and he had done it without obviously selling his soul to the devil. *And* he had done it without turning the race into an acrimonious hate fest. His voting record since that election really was conservative, and he seemed like an obvious choice for McFetridge to make. He was an affable man, and he might even have become a good man eventually if only he had been allowed to do that without having to overcome many obstacles or any stiff resistance. He liked the *idea* of being good.

McFetridge's vetting team had found no skeletons in his closet, but this was because the one skeleton—there was only one significant one—had been carefully hidden twenty years before, and also because McFetridge's vetting team was largely made up of evangelicals. These people were hard-working, and professional, and always on time, and were the nicest people on earth, but the last Calvinists in their respective family trees had died sometime in the mid-nineteenth century, and so their understanding of the doctrine of total depravity had died with them, meaning that their bright and cheerful descendants did not really know what questions to ask, or what a skeleton in a closet would even look like by now. So they missed it.

The oppo research team were not suffering under the same constraints of niceness, and found the problem pretty much right away. They didn't do it in twenty minutes, but they did it pretty fast. Once that file made its way up the chain of command, this occasioned a good deal of debate on how to use the information.

The information they found, and that Billy had kept hidden in a back room for some years, for those who are interested in such things, was that twenty years before, when Billy Jerome was a lowly schlub congressman, he had a buxom staffer named Sheila that he had gotten with child. That child had been well cared for financially, as had his mom, and he was now in his second year at Yale majoring, Billy thought, in some kind of woke studies. He had no idea who his father was, and Billy guessed it was likely he would have had some sort of conniption fit if he ever found out, and thought it best that we not tell him.

His mother knew, and now Billy's opponents in the presidential and vice-presidential showdown also knew. They did not get this information from Sheila, who had been true to her signature on the agreement, but rather from some gossipy former staffers from that by-gone era. They put two and two together, and being cynical the way Christian staffers are not, came up with four.

But what were they to do with this glorious info? This kind of thing was par for the course for a lot of politicians, but not for a guy like Billy Jerome, who had a ninety-eight percent approval rating from the Family Research Council. If this glorious news came out in an opportune way for the Democrats, that could easily seal the deal on the election for them.

There had actually been a council of war on this very subject, at the highest echelons. Brock Tilton was there, naturally, as was Del Martin, and a handful of their top advisors. And the chair of the oppo team was invited in, who was delivering the file on Billy to them.

"So when do we blow this thing up?" one of the advisors said. "That seems to me to be the only question. Now or later?"

Brock Tilton shook his head sharply. "*Not* now. Definitely later. We *use* it now, we reveal it later."

"What do you mean, boss?"

Brock swiveled in his chair and looked hard at Del. "Your debate with him is in two weeks. How are the mock debates coming? And what do you think of him as a debater? You've been watching all the footage, right?"

Del nodded, not liking at all the fact that he was in yet another gunk meeting. It seemed to him that they were all turning into gunk meetings. He wondered briefly why he had never noticed it before. Surely they had not magically turned into gunk meetings just within the last month. Del looked steadily back at Brock.

"He is actually quite good. Quick on his feet, and has a good mastery of facts. I do think I can stay with him, but I have to say he is good at what he does. You all know that. McFetridge picked him for a reason."

"Then we need him to be *less* good on that night. We need him to take a dive. Not too obvious. Just lose a step or two. Give us a few stammering video clips to use in ads. We tell him we know, and the price of our silence is for him to help us out just a *little* bit in that debate."

"You mean you don't want to use this info?" The head of oppo gasped.

"Of course we use it, bozo," Tilton said. "We just tell Billy that we won't. That way he helps us out in the debate, and we get the value of the research later on, I would say about two weeks before the election would be about right. He pays for a silence he does not actually receive. We've been looking for our October surprise. This is it."

Del's stomach was churning. He was about to object, saying that to pull a double cross that way wasn't playing it straight, when one of the advisors said it first. "But . . . to do that, after he agrees to work with us?"

"I don't know who said it first, kid, but politics ain't beanbag."

Del's new conscience saw an opportunity to say something. He *had* to say something, and he was sick about the whole thing.

"I'm not sure he would be so stupid as to agree to cooperate with us. He might not play ball, not because he is a man of integrity, but because he's not a fool. And he is *not* a fool. He knows we would be holding all the cards, and could easily break our word."

"Yep, he knows that. But even if he does the stalwart thing, the fact that he knows that *we* know all about it is like to put him off his game in the debate anyhow. This whole thing is a no-lose proposition."

Brock turned to the oppo research chairman. "Good job. Tell your team good job."

DEL STARTS TO KICK A LITTLE MORE

Keith Everett had been with the Secret Service for about five years, and had excelled there. His current assignment was that of serving on the detail that protected the vice-presidential candidate and his family, an assignment that he had initially accepted with some reluctance. Most of the guys detested serving on the Democratic side of things, not because of politics or character, but mostly because of personalities. The Republicans tended to be every bit as sinful, but nowhere near as entitled. And it was the entitled part that would always get you if you were part of "the help."

At the same time, it was strictly *verboten* in the Service to point out such obvious things, at least verbally, and so the received wisdom among the agents was transmitted from the older generation to the newbies by means of eye rolls and the waggling of eyebrows. This is how Keith had initially developed his distaste for serving on the Democratic side.

And it was also why he was pleasantly surprised by Gina Martin. She was, and there is really no other way to put it, *nice*. Her husband was something of a hard driver, and very fastidious with his staff—that is, the people who reported to him directly. But Del Martin was not a terror to any by-standers—the Secret Service, hotel staff, and other random types who brought him coffee. If you weren't a direct report, he always said *thank you*. But there was still a visible hardness about him. So he hadn't exasperated Keith yet, and his wife was nice.

Keith was built like a couple of fire hydrants, one on top of the other, and the top one was a little bit wider. This was not an accident of nature, although nature had granted him a head start, but rather was diligently maintained by his regular early morning work-outs at a hole-in-the-wall gym he had found a few years before, just the kind he liked. It was an old school gym, with a punching bag and everything. It had *some* new equipment, but was not anything like one of those techno-mart wall-to-wall muscle factories. He detested those. Mirrors everywhere, as though a gym was supposed to be some kind of a satanic and narcissistic fun house.

And it was during his early morning workout sessions that he had first met Larry Locke. They had first passed casually a few times and exchanged pleasantries. After that, they got into a few conversations and discovered a mutual likemindedness. Then they started spotting one another occasionally on the bench press, and it had evolved to the point where they were now work-out partners, at least when they were both there. Keith's travel schedule meant that he frequently was not there, but they got on famously whenever he was.

And on this particular morning, Keith had a story for Larry, which had happened to him on the previous day. He was both encouraged and mystified by it.

"What happened?" Larry asked. And so Keith told him—there were some interruptions, but when the whole story was out, it went like this:

"Agent Everett," Gina had said, "may I speak to you for a moment?"

"Certainly, ma'am," he said, and stepped over toward her.

She spoke to him cautiously, but not like she was whispering a secret or anything like that. At the same time, she spoke in a way that seemed natural enough, but not in a way that the agents in the next room could hear. And if they did hear bits and pieces of it, they would think it was totally normal. Which it wasn't.

"This might seem random to you," she said, "and I apologize if it seems a bit personal. But picking up on a few odd things here and there, I wanted to ask you if you were an evangelical."

"Yes, ma'am," he said, grinning slightly. "I am glad it is noticeable, at least if what you noticed wasn't terrible."

Gina stood silent for a moment, and Keith was thinking about asking if that were all, and going back to his spot in the corner. But he noticed that she seemed like she was going back and forth in her mind about whether to say anything more, and then saw that she was going to say something in a minute, if he would just *give* her a minute. So he just waited.

"I . . . I think that my husband has recently become . . . one of those . . . one of *you*, I mean. Sorry. I don't know what it means, and I have really no idea how to respond or what to think of it, but I . . . I am worried about him. The campaign is, um, not a God-fearing place."

"No, ma'am," he said. "It isn't."

"Is there a way you might throw him a rope? Let him know that *somebody* there understands it? I am concerned he is headed for an epic collision with . . . with everybody else there."

And Keith was thinking to himself something like *you have no idea*. But what he said was, "I am glad you told me, ma'am. This does explain a number of things."

"You've noticed a difference then?"

"Well, yes, I have. But so has everybody else, or virtually everyone. But no one has any idea that it could be anything like this. The most common theory is that the campaign doctor was experimenting with the uppers again."

"Oh, no," Gina said. "Just the opposite. That was one of the first things I noticed after . . . *after*. He quit taking all those pills the next day. I found them in the garbage."

And so Keith promised her that he would keep an eye out, and that if there was something he could say that was consistent with the strict protocols that the Service had regarding personal interactions with the candidates and their families, he would do it. Gina seemed genuinely reassured and relieved.

And just that afternoon, an opportunity had opened up, like there was a higher power at work. Keith was standing at the side of the same room where the candidate would meet with pollsters and consultants, at least when they were there, and Del was at the other end of the room, working through a sheaf of papers. It was some of the background material he needed to master before his upcoming debate with Billy Jerome. The two men were alone together for a couple of minutes before Del noticed. But as soon as he noticed, he gave a little start and put the sheaf of papers down and stood up.

Putting his hands in his pockets, he walked over toward Keith.

"Keith," he said, coming right to the point—and not having any use for the Agent Everett stuff—"do you believe in God?"

"Yes, sir," Keith smiled. "And in Jesus Christ, His only begotten Son."

Del looked around the room like he was about to sell some classified material to a swarthy Russian named Oleg. He looked back at Keith. "I think we are the only two here."

"Yes, sir," Keith said. "I believe that is correct."

"Okay," Del said. "So here's the problem. You guys know how to bustle us into limousines. You know how to push us down to the asphalt when the car backfires. You know how to jump in between the candidate and some aggressive member of the public. Hats off to you all."

"Thank you, I'm sure," Keith said.

"But it seems to me that we might have a situation coming up where I and my family might need protection in a way that I suspect was not covered by any training manual that you have ever seen. No offense, but this is a weird one."

When Keith finished laying everything out for Larry, Larry nodded his astonishment. "The good senator wasn't lying to you. This *is* a weird one."

CHAPTER 7

More Unexpected Guests

DINNER FOR FOUR

Eve was busy that morning, checking the senator's travel schedule back in Montana, and she found herself making more mistakes than was usual. She shook her head, trying to get her mind back on her work. The temptation was to think about what she saw coming with Larry and Jill instead.

She did not belong to a theological tradition that believed that the prophetic gifts were still extent, and so she did not attribute her foresight to anything supernatural. Rather she attributed it to her having eyes in her head. A couple days after Larry had made his first visit to the senator's office, he was back again, almost as soon as the office opened. Eve stood up as she saw him coming, made a point of making knowing eye contact with him as she proceeded to make herself scarce down the hallway. That left the path open to Jill's office, and as her door was halfway open, Larry immediately filled it.

"Morning," he said.

"Good morning," she said, startled, and standing up immediately.

"I was wondering if I might ask you out for dinner, either tonight or tomorrow night, whichever would be most convenient for you."

Jill swallowed with some difficulty. "Um," she said. "I would like that . . . either night would work fine."

"Well, since I am eager to go out with you, let's make it tonight."

As first dates go, it really was a success. Jill was pleased that he appeared to be genuinely interested in her, and he was a *very* interesting person to talk to. Larry was also very pleased with their evening out. They talked in detail about politics, and about theology, and about music, and movies. He found out, in the course of their rambling discussion, that her theological views mapped onto his almost exactly, and moreover, she appeared to be a sweetheart. An actual nice person, living in the D.C. area. He was very impressed. He had found out she was a Christian during his first visit to the office, which is why he was willing to ask her out, but Christians come in all flavors, and some of them wouldn't pair nicely with the flavor that Larry knew himself to be. He was most gratified, and thought that this was something that needed to be pushed along.

The only other eventful thing about that first date was that on the way to the restaurant Jill had saved Larry's life, and so perhaps that is something that should be mentioned. They were standing at a crosswalk that had just gone to "don't walk," and

Larry said, "Excuse me while I pull up the address. I made our reservations earlier, but neglected to save the directions."

"Sure thing," Jill had said.

So while they were standing there at the crosswalk, Larry was busy with his phone. Jill was meditating on the fact that the second button down from the top of his shirt was right at her eye level, and she was marveling at the novelty of the experience. It made her feel all kinds of ways. She glanced up and broke away from her meditations for a moment, just in time to notice a car coming their way that was dangerously close to the curb, and going way too fast. She shouted, jumping back, and grabbing Larry's collar as she did so. They both fell backward into a hedge that flanked the sidewalk on the other side of it, and Larry did a backward somersault through the hedge, and came up on his feet on the other side. They had been the only two at the crosswalk, which meant the car lurched across the sidewalk, right where they had been, careened back into the street, and veered left, disappearing in about ten seconds. It was not a *hit-and-run*, but rather an *almost-hit-and-run-even-faster.*

Larry reached down and took Jill's hand, and lifted her out of the hedge easily.

She found her feet, brushed herself off. "I am most grateful to you," Larry said. "That was close."

"I am grateful I was able to *move* you," she said. "I can't believe I actually did it. Unlike how you lifted me out of the hedge just now. I felt like you were picking up a piece of cotton batting."

In short, the date part of the first date was successful, and the exciting part of the first date had not been *too* exciting.

But however gratified he was with their first date, he had to admit later that their second date, one that happened about a week later, was far more memorable. Larry opened the door to the Sautéed Onion for Jill, and she made her way into the restaurant, with Larry joining her at the hostess stand just a moment later. Larry, through long experience, waited a moment before he spoke, giving the hostess a chance to catch her breath.

"Table for two?" she finally managed. *Table for three is more like it*, she was thinking.

"Yes, that is right," he said, and nodded when she said, "Follow me, please." She led them to a table that was set for four that was on a raised platform next to a broad bay window. "Oh, how lovely," Jill said. A moment later, she added, "If we both sit on this side, we will have a wonderful view of the river."

"Sure thing," Larry said.

And they had been seated at their table just barely long enough to get their menus when Cody and Helen came through the front door. They both looked left and right, and then hurry-walked to the left, looking like they were going to try to head straight through the restaurant and out the back door. About a third of the way there, Cody suddenly changed his mind, turned around, glanced back at the front door, grabbed Helen's hand, pulled back an empty chair at Larry and Jill's table, seated Helen in it firmly, stepped behind her, and sat down at the next chair, which was also empty.

"Please pardon us," Cody said to the startled Jill, and the presumably startled Larry, even though he didn't look startled. "I will explain ourselves thoroughly in just a moment, and apologize even more handsomely. In the meantime, may I borrow your menus?"

Larry had decided in that instant that he was going to trust Cody, who looked vaguely familiar, and he nodded. He then crooked his finger at a passing waiter and asked for two more menus, which appeared promptly.

"Am I right in assuming that it would be good for all of us to be busy with noses in our menus over the next few minutes?"

"Yes," Cody said, almost out of breath. "That would be very good. Proper, in fact."

As they were examining their menus, and Jill, quick on the uptake, was talking loudly about the salmon, and gesturing, Larry noticed—as he was seated in a way that would enable him to notice—two men walk in the front door, and straight past the hostess stand. She said, somewhat feebly, "Were you expecting to meet . . . ?" but by that time they were headed toward the back door next to the kitchen. A moment later, they blew out that door, the way that Cody and Helen had almost gone.

"Your instincts were strong," Helen said to Cody. "My debts to you are increasing."

Larry leaned forward, and bumped the table as he did so. A few of the water glasses sloshed. "Sorry," he said. "That always happens. But I will make you two a deal. I would like to buy you dinner in exchange for some sort of *explanation*. Given the look of those two thugs, you might want to lie to us, but I would still like to feed you and hear some kind of explanation anyhow."

At that moment the waiter appeared. Cody looked at Helen, who nodded. She didn't know what Cody was going to tell these people, but she was starting to trust him more and more. And besides, she suddenly realized that she was famished.

"Well, perhaps we should begin with introductions," Cody said. "My name is Cody. Cody Vance. This is Helen, Dr. Helen Greene." With this, Cody looked straight at Larry for the first time, started back in his seat, and exclaimed, "and we have met before. *You* are Larry Locke. I heard you lecture two months ago, and you were kind enough to sign my book."

Larry nodded. "Yes, I am the one. I remember meeting you, in fact. You teach at Liberty? Is that right?"

Cody turned to Jill, who extended her hand, and they shook. "I am Jill Stevens," she said. "I am *not* famous." Helen did the same, and it initially seemed that they were done with the odd coincidences, when Larry said, "Dr. Helen Greene . . . are you a climatologist?" She nodded, as though she were aware of what was coming, which she halfway was. But she didn't know why or how she could know. She didn't know Larry Locke from Adam. Her puzzled look drew an explanation from Larry.

"My book is called *Ecochondriacs*. I suspect we might be on different sides of the climate change issue. There is a section in my chapter ten where I, um, critique a paper you submitted to *The Journal of Climate Change*."

This was a polite way of putting it. Larry had actually gone through her paper with a weed whacker, the kind with metal blades.

Helen looked down at the table, somewhat embarrassed. "We were no doubt on different sides, although I am afraid I was unaware of your critique. In that world, my old world, we were taught to ignore all of that like it was the yapping of small dogs in the distance. But my views have been undergoing some, um, revision. I am not exactly in the position of switching sides. It is more like I have been chased over here. But I am starting to like it." She looked at Cody, shyly.

Cody looked back at her. "Do you mind if I request some help from these good folks? All we have been doing thus far is running, and running is not a long term plan."

She nodded. She had liked Jill instantly, and she was even cautiously warm to Larry, not having seen him stand up yet.

"Now you *really* have me curious," Larry said. Jill nodded her agreement. *Curious* was a radical understatement.

Cody turned to Helen. "You tell them the first part," he said. "I'll pick it up from where you hopped in my car."

And so she did. She described her position with the international task force on climate change, how she got the damning email, the attempted hit, how she ran out the front door and into the life of Cody Vance. Larry's eyes were wide open. Jill had taken her hand when she had gotten to the part where she had shot her assassin, and when she was done Larry whistled through his teeth. Then they both looked at Cody.

He said, "We have been driving around aimlessly ever since. They almost got us twice since then, counting tonight. The first time was a close call last night. But the people on our tail now seem to be a bit more competent than the first group who broke into Helen's condo. I am assuming higher levels of competence because I have no idea how they managed to track us here tonight. They pulled into the parking lot just as we were coming through the front door. I recognized their car from last night. I just happened to turn around at the right moment. It wasn't the car, I don't think, because we didn't park in the restaurant lot."

Larry leaned forward again, and sloshed more water. "Do you still have that thumb drive?" Cody and Helen both nodded.

"The first thing we need to do," Larry said, "is get copies of that hot property made. They need to be chasing five or six copies of the damning emails, not one. There is a computer shop in a mall right near here. We can hit that right after the salmon."

And Jill broke in. "And there is a public library two miles that way down this strip. We can use the computers there to make the copies."

They all visited together until the salmon came, and all found that they were liking each other very much. When they were almost done with their meal, Helen commented that she still found it hard to believe that anybody could order someone else murdered over a *political* issue. "I still haven't gotten my mind around it," she said.

Larry smiled at her, somewhat grimly. "If they had gotten you, you wouldn't have been the first. Actually, it is quite possible that you wouldn't have been the first this month."

"That can't be possible," Helen gasped, but then she saw the look in his eye. "Cody here made one of those stupid Arkancide jokes a few days ago, but that was a *joke*. I think. You are talking about this seriously! *Are* you?"

Larry looked at her, with something like compassion in his eyes. He glanced over at Cody before speaking.

"Do you believe the United States is a powerful country, a great empire?"

"Why are you changing the subject?"

Larry shook his head. "Not changing the subject at all. More political power flows through this town than flowed through Nineveh, Babylon, Rome, and the courts of the Mongol kings all put together. And so if political assassinations and hits were not routinely conducted in our midst for the sake of maintaining that power, it would be the very first time in history that such a thing has ever happened. As fond as I am of our country, I don't think we can assume that nobody is periodically encouraged to leave the land of the breathing for political reasons."

Helen was staring at him, open-mouthed. She suddenly wheeled on Cody.

"Do *you* think that too?"

Cody grinned at her. "Well, I admit that I used to think that way back before we got acquainted. Maybe not as hard core as Larry here. But since we have become such close friends, we have successfully evaded various attempts on your life, right? And all for political reasons, right? So what I used to *think*, it would be fair to say that now I *know*."

"We need to go," she said. "I need to think."

JILL ANSWERS A QUESTION

They made it to the mall in just a few minutes. "Why doesn't Cody go in and get some more thumb drives," Larry said. "I am going to go over there by that nice little tree and act as a sentry. Keep your phones out. We'll both be back in just a few minutes. Keep the doors locked."

The two women waited quietly in the parking lot, and because it was cool out, they had kept the car running.

"I have a question for you," Helen said suddenly from the back seat.

"Sure," Jill replied, turning around to see Helen a bit better.

"Okay, I am in a bit of a paradigm jumble, and I know it. People I have looked up to for years are trying to have me killed, and people I have despised for years are trying to save my life, and not just out of a sense of duty. But over the last decade or so, I have not just despised this second lot of people for their supposed evil, but also for being morons. But as I have spent time with Cody, and now with you and Larry, I find that all of you are both nice and educated."

Jill laughed. "And we take showers."

"I know, this sounds really bad. Sorry. But that was the frame of mind I had the night before my boss sent some men over to shoot me. I am just describing it for you. And that frame of mind is now hopelessly tangled up. But occasionally an intelligible question works its way to the top of my brain tangle, and so I grab it."

"So what is your question?" Jill asked.

"I want to know how Steven Lee, a man who dedicated his life to saving the planet, could just flip a switch and send men to kill me."

"I think you are asking the question the wrong way," Jill said.

"What do you mean?"

"I mean that *you* thought he was dedicating his life to saving the planet. You are on the run now because you received a batch of emails that revealed that *he* never really thought that, at least not for many years now. It is only a contradiction if he has an actual moral center."

Helen sat, pondering for a minute. "But it is *such* a contradiction."

"Is he an atheist?"

Helen sat up straight, surprised by the question. "Well, certainly. Everyone at the center was, including me. And before you say anything rude, I probably still am."

"Then there is no such thing as contradiction. There is no God, and Steven Lee can do just as he pleases. In fact, I would want to argue that he is being far more consistent with his atheism than you were being."

Helen was quiet for a moment. "I guess I am not surprised that you would say that. But why do you say that?"

Jill turned the heater down. "There are atheists who try very hard to conform to a particular moral code. You were one of them. But it is an arbitrary moral code, suspended in mid-air. You cannot answer any questions about *why* it has any moral authority whatever. That means that whatever moral code you adopt is adopted 'just because.'"

Helen was quiet for a bit longer this time. "But when I got up in the morning and went to work, I really *was* doing it to save the planet. And I was fighting people like you who didn't care about saving the planet. I really was."

Jill turned around in her seat even further. "Right. I don't doubt that this is what you were doing at all. I am simply saying that you couldn't answer any questions about *why* you were doing it, or why anybody else should care the same way you did. You just took it as self-evident that they *should* care, and that they were bad people for not caring."

The two women sat in silence for several minutes, until Jill picked up the thread again. Jill had used that moment to recollect the way her apologetics teacher used to talk about it.

"If there is no moral standard that overarches all of us, to which all of us are equally obligated, then there is no such thing as good or bad. The absence of that transcendent moral authority means that all of our 'moral' choices are simply preferences. You like grape nuts, somebody else doesn't like grape nuts."

"You mean . . . ?" Helen said, and then stopped.

"Yes, I do, if I am guessing your next question rightly. I mean that if there is no objective moral authority overarching you and Steven Lee, then your desire to save the planet is just a personal preference, and his desire to milk those people who want to save the planet is just a personal preference. And neither one is superior to the other. They both just *are*."

And then Helen blurted out, suddenly close to tears, and not knowing where that impulse came from. "But what he tried to do to me was *evil*."

Jill nodded, and her voice was filled with sympathy. "Yes. Yes, it was. And that is one of the central reasons I say there is a God. If there is no God, then you and Steven Lee are just two bits of protoplasm that got in each other's way. Which is obviously incorrect. You are much more than that."

Helen sat back in her seat. "Thank you," she said. "Thanks. I think I am beginning to see what you people are talking about."

And with that, they saw Larry headed toward the car, and Cody angling across the parking lot to meet him. They headed out to the library, where Cody went in and made five copies of the email thread. Cody and Helen took two, and Larry and Jill three.

"What I want to do is put two of these in places where they will be made public if anything happens to us," Larry said. "This last one is the ball we want to put in play. We have to do that in a way that cannot be shut down or ignored."

"All right," Helen said. "And we will be trying to figure out something similar with ours." They all exchanged phone numbers, and promised to be in close touch.

Larry drove them back to the restaurant, and drove through the parking lot twice so that Cody and Helen could look to see if the car of the men pursuing them was still there. It wasn't.

Larry then dropped them off at Cody's rental car, waited for them to drive off, and then drove Jill home. "Well," he said. "I can't promise that every date will be nearly as exciting, but I would like to do this again. I would like to see you more . . . a lot more."

Jill nodded. "Okay," she said. "I would enjoy that too."

CHAPTER 8

Asteroids

HASANI IN A PANIC

Hugh Hasani—erstwhile assassination coordinator—was in a state of high panic, and in his case, the effects happened to be salutary. Many ordinary folks have noticed that the onset of panic has the unfortunate effect of scattering their wits. Hugh, whose wits were usually scattered already, discovered much to his great surprise that his panic was out there gathering up all his wits, and helping them all to walk in a straight line.

When he had first discovered that Steven Lee had taken the hit job away from him, and given it to that Rocco character, he had been dismayed. But most of his dismay on that point was simply over his loss of a client, and the resultant loss of revenue. Simple. But then, two days later, when he called the hospital to find out how Maurice was doing, what he had found out was

that Maurice had died suddenly during the night, causes un-
known. This does not usually happen as the result of a wound
to the leg. Filled with sudden foreboding, he immediately tried
to call Leon.

No one picked up after repeated tries, and so eventually he
called Leon's mother. She was *so* distraught . . . apparently Leon
had gone out late the night before, still depressed from whatever
had happened at work the other morning, and had jumped off
a bridge. He was declared dead at the emergency room. Hugh
stammered out his condolences, got off the phone, and started
hopping around his office.

He had heard *stories* about Rocco, and when he had first heard
them, he took sort of reflected pride in them. He and Rocco
were both in the direct action business, no fooling around. But
now that "no fooling around" bit seemed more ominous. Rocco
hated loose ends. He wouldn't just take the job, he would also
clean up after the previous slipshod workers. "*I* have to be on
that list," Hugh thought. "*Why* did I have to go and mention
Rocco to Lee? Rocco wouldn't bump me off just to keep things
tidy, and . . . yes, yes, he actually would."

This continued on for about five minutes until Hugh started
to get tired and out of breath—he was not in great physical
shape, and so he sat down at his desk. It, like the rest of the
office, was in tatters. If decorators had terms for this kind of
thing, they would probably narrow it down to a choice between High Disheveled and Early Hand Grenade. He looked
gloomily out over darkened room. "I am *done*. I have nothing
to negotiate with."

"Unless . . ." he thought, sitting up a little straighter. "Unless *I* had that Helen character. If I had her, I could name my price, and the very first part of my price would be that of not following in the unhappy footsteps of Maurice and Leon."

Then he slumped in the chair again. *How was he supposed to get Helen?*

Leon had reported to him that she had been in the passenger seat of a dark Tahoe, with Maryland plates. Who on that street owned a Tahoe? He should be able to find that out. He should probably start with whoever lived right across the street. Helen's apartment was right near the end of a cul de sac, and it is unlikely that she could have caught a ride from anyone "downstream." Checking that out would be the only footwork that would be needed. The rest of it could be computer work, and he was good at hacking. He knew how to hack things.

By the following afternoon, he knew that the man across the street was named Cody Vance, that he taught at Liberty, and that the neighbors hadn't seen him for a few days. The neighbors assumed that Hugh was a cop, because cops had been around a few days before asking the same sort of questions. They were consequently most helpful, and more than a little curious. "Any sign of Helen yet?" one of the women had asked. Hugh tried to answer her in a gruff and official way which might have given him completely away if she had been paying much attention to it. "No, no," he said. "Very curious," he added.

And by that evening, he had what he thought he needed. He had gotten into Vance's email account, and had also cracked his text messages. Those text messages confirmed that Helen and Cody were together, and that they were still running, and it appeared they were running nowhere in particular. But then he ran into a wall. After this point, he had no way of chasing them, or finding them, or anything. However, the panic that was coursing through his veins was serving as makeshift adrenaline, and he suddenly had an idea. He could *pretend* that he had Helen and Cody.

But who should he pretend it *to*? Rocco? No, that man was a hardshell assassin, and would see right through a bluff like that. But Rocco was the one who was going to kill him deader than Leon, or perhaps Maurice. The ruse that he supposedly had Helen and Cody was information that needed to get to Rocco somehow, and in a believable way.

When he had been going through Cody's texts, there was a group text thread that he hadn't read, thinking it must be irrelevant if other people were involved in it, but a wave of second thoughts came over him. He went back and looked, and a wave of glee almost drowned his panic, almost. There he was, big as all get out. Larry Locke. Larry Locke was Hugh's very own personal antichrist. And then Jill Stevens? Stevens, Stevens. *That* was the name of that senator's tall but fetching staffer, not that she was Hugh's type. She was the one he had to go through whenever he had to set up a phone call with Hart, for those occasional times when he finally got up the energy to put the screws to her.

He stewed about it for several hours, and enough of an idea began to take shape that he thought he had been struck by the muse of dirty deals. There was no telling when Rocco was going to send somebody around to tidy up the loose end that his mother had once called Hughie.

He would create a false account and text Larry Locke with the information that he had Helen and Cody, and would Locke be interested in arranging a ransom payment? Hugh was fairly certain that Rocco would be into their accounts also, and that would let Rocco know that he had Helen and Cody in his custody. He, Hugh, was not to be trifled with.

Hugh thought that and then remembered Rocco's face, and quavered a little bit. The only problem he could see would be if the real Helen or Cody, running around loose, texted Larry or Jill about meeting or something. After pondering a bit, Hugh thought he could go into Larry and Jill's accounts and just block Cody and Helen. That would fix *that*.

LARRY LIBERATES MARSHA

When Ken had first told Larry about his rumored theory that somebody was blackmailing certain inconsistent votes out of Sen. Marsha Hart, he had also said that the people doing it had been quite deft. In other words, they had not overplayed their hand, which would have made the good senator a vulnerable primary target back in Montana. In this speculation, he was right about the effect it was having, but wrong about the cause. The cause was something more like simple incompetence.

For the person with the dirt on her was none other than Hugh Hasani, and the dirt was located in the offices of Earth

Fight. And by this point it goes without saying that they had not been clever enough to find the dirt themselves—*that* had been given to them by an overworked staffer at the DNC who had needed to get a few things off his desk. I use the phrase *his desk* advisedly because this staffer, now going by Heather, was already transitioning, with fake breasts and everything, and to apply the old pronoun might entail legal difficulties for, as the Victorians would have put it, the present writer. But the legal team for Satiric Writers Guild is a crackerjack team in every respect, and so I have made the decision to simply proceed. Let it stand. Stet. Whatever the editors may say about it, *stet*. Where was I?

Right. He had a pile of dirt on his desk, and he needed to offload some of it, and he had a cousin who worked for Earth Fight, and so that is how Earth Fight became a very important group of people in Sen. Hart's eyes, although she didn't even know who they were, and this made them even more important figures in their own eyes. They would certainly have been willing to demand that she roll over on every single vote, but they kept getting distracted by other stuff. And so, being stymied by their own laziness, they were thus failing to put the squeeze on her except at intermittent intervals. The effect was almost professional, and that is what had excited Ken's grudging admiration. It was, alas, a misplaced admiration.

Larry had been thinking hard about what to do with the emails that he was now carrying around. They were burning a hole in his pocket, not unlike that genuine silver dollar his grandfather had once given him when he was a kid. In this state, for some reason his thoughts had turned to the upcoming vice-presidential debates. He had met Billy Jerome several times, and thought that he *might* be willing to produce the emails in the middle of the debate, but after some thought he decided it was too risky. They would think, all his advisors would think, that it was a risky stunt to pull in a veep debate, and that it could easily blow up on them. And if they thought it was too risky for them, then it would be too risky for Larry to attempt going through Jerome. He corrected himself immediately. *For Larry and Jill. Too risky for Larry and Jill. That seemed to fit somehow.*

But as he was settling in to ponder it some more, his phone in his breast pocket chirruped at him. He pulled it out, tapped the screen, and his eyes got wide. "What?" Jill asked him.

The text message simply said, "We have Helen and Cody. Listen to the voice memo if you would like to learn how to get them back."

So Larry poked at the little arrow that would play the memo, poking it three times. He started to say something about his stupid phone, but Jill interrupted. "I think it has to do with the size of your finger," she said. "Let me." She reached over, touched the screen, and the message began to play.

"My name is Asteroid. We have Helen and Cody," the voice said. "If you would like me to send proof of that, I am willing to do so, but I am also happy to proceed straight to negotiations. My name is not really Asteroid."

"Ask him for the proof," Jill said. "Buy some time. But in the meantime, I think I know who that is."

"All right," Larry said, and typed in, "Send your proof."

Then he turned to Jill, an activity he found himself wanting to do more and more. "How could you possibly know who it is?"

"He said *neggotiashuns*, with a hard g and a hard t," Jill said. "I heard him speak once at a rally I had to attend. Same there. That is his own private shibboleth. And I have talked to him on the phone a few times also. He has called the senator from time to time. *That* is Hugh Hasani, from Earth Fight. He is not the brightest bulb in the pack."

"And I know right where the Earth Fight offices are. I drive by them on the way to work, and I sing imprecatory psalms whenever I do."

Jill stood up. "Well, let's go then."

Whoa, Larry thought. *A woman of action.*

She was standing at the door, car keys in hand, looking back. Larry hopped up and followed her. They both knew, without talking about it, that they couldn't call the cops because Helen had no way of preventing her well-placed enemies from steamrolling a local police department. To involve the police would be tantamount to giving up. They couldn't really talk to the police until they had a plan in place for publishing the emails in a way that could not be spiked.

It was after business hours when they pulled into the rundown little strip mall where Earth Fight's solitary office—international, national, and local offices, depending on who they were trying to impress, all rolled into one—was located. It was after business hours, but not yet fully dark. Larry told Jill to wait in the car while he walked around to the back. The office was three in from the end, and so Larry was able easily to count the back doors. After he had done so, he noticed an Earth Fight sign posted on the door for UPS drivers, so it turned out he needn't have bothered with the counting. He took one look at the lock, and went back to get Jill. When the two of them got to the back door again, he took out a credit card, looked at Jill, and grinned.

"I do not have a criminal background, just so you know. I am simply mechanically inclined."

Jill smiled back at him and said nothing. She hoped her smile was not of the adoring variety. Larry had the door open in about thirty seconds, and stepped across the threshold. He stood in the hallway for a moment, waiting for an alarm to sound, but nothing happened.

He walked down the central hallway toward the waiting room, and stood still for a moment. "This place is a *pit*," he said, as if to no one in particular. Jill had turned into a side room momentarily, and looked both this way and that for any place where a couple of prisoners might be kept. Nothing there. But on the left side of that room sat a wobbly card table with a couple of dirty rags on it, and on top of them was a crescent wrench, about a foot long. For no particular reason other than personal safety, she picked it up, and hefted it in her hand. *Nice.*

The main offices were down the hall further, also on the right. Larry had gone down that hallway, but turned left to look over the waiting room first. He was saving the office area for last.

But when he had said that the place was a *pit*, one of the consequences of his comment was that he awakened Hugh Hasani, who had been asleep at his desk. About an hour earlier he had finished a Cup o' Ramen, which was a typical dinner for him, and having worn himself out with all the thinking and figuring about how to steer clear of Rocco, he then laid his head down on the desk for a quick nap. He sat up quickly and quietly, just in time to make out Larry's profile, just before Larry turned away from him to go into the waiting room. *Larry Locke.* He had seen that man multiple times on YouTube, where he always made a point of making some bile-filled comment, which he always signed HH. But that profile was unmistakable. *That* was Larry Locke. His enemy had walked into his lair. He would figure out what to do with the body later.

His right-hand drawer was already open, and it was where he kept his 9mm, which he picked up as he stood. He stepped around his desk and walked silently toward Larry, gun outstretched and at the ready. Larry had gone all the way into the waiting room and stood still for a moment. He was looking around, first at the front door, and then to the left, where a couple of closets were.

Hugh stepped across the hallway and stood in the wide doorway into the waiting room. He quietly and cautiously drew a bead halfway between Larry's shoulder blades. Hugh was a decent shot, but this would be impossible to miss. Larry's shoulder blades seemed like they were a yard apart.

Jill, for her part, had come out of the side room she had been in, and was walking down the hallway, crescent wrench in her right hand. She looked up just as Hugh stepped just inside the waiting room and stopped.

Now, Jill was an athletic woman. Her principal sport had been volleyball, but she had also played a mean game of softball back in her day. She was a decent fielder, but her real strength was at the plate.

So without any reflection at all, she leapt forward, shifting both hands to her little crescent wrench of a bat. Her swing was angled slightly up, as though she were going for the fence. As she connected, she saw that Hugh had been just about to shoot an unsuspecting Larry in the back. The wrench made a satisfying *thwack*, almost as good as in the movies, and Hugh went forward onto his face. It was as though someone just pushed over an upright railroad tie, and the sound of him hitting the floor was also similar.

Larry spun around at the *thwack* and the *thump*, and looked down on a deeply unconscious Hugh. "Well, well," he said, "It appears that I owe you my deepest thanks. A second time." *What a woman*, he was thinking.

After a few seconds, he asked, "Did you see anything in that back room we could tie him up with? Their office staff can deal with him in the morning."

"Just a sec," Jill said. She darted back to the place where she had picked up the crescent wrench, left it there on the card table, and picked up a roll of duct tape that was on the window sill. She was back with Larry in about two minutes. "Here," she said. Larry in the meantime had checked Hugh's pulse, which was steady enough, took the duct tape, and promptly trussed him up in a way calculated to keep him from moving at all. "That should do it." Hugh was still unconscious when he was done. "You must have sent him into the middle of next week," he said.

When he stood up, he asked her, "Have we checked all the rooms, all the doors? These doors are closets. No basement steps, nothing like that?"

"No, this is it," she replied. "The back room, the office with the desks there, and the waiting room here. No Helen and no Cody."

Larry was now musing. Jill was thinking to herself that this was no time for musing.

"We need to get out of here," she whispered at him. "We got the information we wanted. I don't think he has them. He just wanted us to think he did."

He shook his head. "Not everything we wanted. Not yet. I need to check on something Ken told me about."

With that he walked carefully over into the office to a file cabinet that was in the corner, right behind Hugh's desk, and Jill noticed, again not for the first time, how he walked like a cat. A great jungle cat, but a cat nonetheless. "What are you doing?" she said, following him.

"A long shot, but I would feel really bad about myself if I didn't check. And we know her last name begins with an H, so I shouldn't have to go rummaging through the whole file cabinet."

"Maybe when we are safely out of here, you will explain yourself to me in a way that makes some kind of sense."

"Happy to," Larry said, and pulled out the top drawer. And there, about a third of the way back, was a thick file labeled *Hart*. "Ah, pay dirt," he said, and lifted the whole thing out.

He grinned at Jill, and she grinned back, not knowing why. "We can go now," he said. "Judging from the looks of this office, these people are not likely to have an organized set of back ups for anything. I think we can consider your boss, the good senator, to be someone who is now officially in the clear."

JILL'S EXASPERATION

It was the morning after Jill's adventure with Larry at the offices of Earth Fight. The office of Sen. Hart had only been open for fifteen minutes, and Jill and Eve the only ones there. Jill was looking at Eve in exasperation. Unlike most instances of exasperation, she thought she might even be almost enjoying it. She was flirting with enjoying it.

But Jill wasn't exasperated with Eve, but rather with herself, which Eve could see easily enough. And so she waited for Jill to speak.

"Do you know what my problem is with that man?"

"Besides the obvious?" Eve asked.

Jill ignored her and continued. "My problem with that man is that he affects me in ways that go clean contrary to what any reasonable person might be able to guess or anticipate. Do you know how many times I have saved that man's life? Two! I have saved his life *twice*. And do you know what I have wanted to do both times?"

Eve sat quietly, smiling.

"*Both* times I wanted to throw myself into his arms afterwards and say something like 'my hero!' Is that sensible?"

"No," Eve said. "Not at all sensible. Do you want to know what it means?"

"No," Jill muttered. "I do *not* wish to know what it means." *I already know what it means. It means I am a goner.* With that she made her way back to her office, and unloaded her briefcase. The last thing she hauled out was the file on her boss that Larry had retrieved from Hugh's filing cabinet.

They had talked a good long bit about what to do about it, or with it, and they both went back and forth several times. Their options were to destroy the file—Larry had a shredder at his office—or to give it to the senator with an explanation. After a great deal of discussion, they had finally decided to do the latter, and that is why Jill had the file with her. She was going to give it to the senator as soon as she came in, which Jill thought should be any minute now.

Once they had made their decision, Larry had walked her through how she ought to explain herself when she delivered the file. She really liked how he walked her through it, and really agreed with his approach, and appreciated his care for her, and it made her feel cozy all over, and then she found herself hissing at herself again. *He has asked you out on precisely two dates, and that is all, Jill-person.*

She heard the front doors opening, guessed it was the senator, and stood up to take a peek out. Yep. There she was. Jill went back to her desk, picked up the file, and fidgeted for a couple minutes, allowing time for the senator to deposit her stuff and get settled. This is what they did every morning, so there was nothing unusual about it. Except for the payload that Jill was about to deliver. She had no idea how her boss would react. No idea. Would she get angry? Be offended? Grateful? What?

With those questions rattling around in her mind, Jill took a deep breath, picked up the file, and walked down the hall. She tapped on the door like she always did, went in, and sat down like she always did.

The two women exchanged a few comments about the weather, and about the busy schedule that day, and there was enough back and forth to tell that the senator was in something of a glum mood. *Oh great*, Jill thought.

"I have something out of the ordinary for you today," she said.

"What is it?" the senator asked, jotting down a note while she talked.

"Well, I can't explain it without it appearing to you that I know more than I do. But I don't. I don't know more than I do, if you follow me."

"No, I don't," the senator said, looking up, interested.

"It's like this," Jill said. And she got up and deposited the file on the senator's desk. "That is a file on you that I have obtained. It would be best if we did not go into how I obtained it. I will only say that my conscience is clean on the point. I have not read the file, and have not even looked in it."

"A file on *me*?"

"Yes," Jill said. "And here is where some scuttlebutt comes in, and I am sure you have heard some of the same things that I have. Some people have said that some of your, um, votes were coerced out of you by some people who were threatening you with some information they had about you."

At first Senator Hart flushed, and then went more than a little pale. Jill couldn't tell if she was upset or relieved.

"I have good reason to believe that the people threatening you, if there were any such people, will not be doing so any more. And if they did, I have reason to believe that the only way they could act on any of their threats is all contained in that file there. Which you may dispose of however you see fit. If there was anything to the rumors, which I have no way of knowing, I believe you can be done worrying about it now."

Marsha Hart was sitting quietly, and finally said, in a very soft voice, "Thank you. This is a great relief."

"I'm glad," Jill said, and made as if to go. "You have an opening this afternoon at one. Should we have our regular session then?"

"Yes, please," the senator said. "I need some time to think."

As Jill walked over to the door, she spoke again, very softly. "Jill?"

Jill turned in the doorway. "Yes?"

"Jill, I think the world of you. You need to know that the things in the file were mostly just embarrassing. But once they had me on the hook, I couldn't figure out what to *do*. And there are two votes that I am really ashamed of. I don't know what to do about that."

Jill grinned. "Well, the first thing I would do is shred that file. And the second thing is that revised versions of those two bills are coming up again next month. I suggest that you surprise everyone with your first vote, and then request to become a co-sponsor on the second bill. Surprise everyone again."

"That would be pleasant. But what would I *say*?"

"Say that you changed your mind." And Jill was out the door.

ANOTHER APPROACH

Larry sat up in bed suddenly. *That was it.* What to do with Helen's emails. The thought had come to him unbidden in that drowsy doze between sleeping and waking. It was a long shot, but as far as he could see it was the only good shot they had. They could always get the emails published, and that easily enough, but Larry also knew that if any conservative outfit did it, the story would be yawned out of existence. And nobody but a true-blue conservative outfit would even touch it. In fact, he knew there were even some true blues that wouldn't do it. The crazies would be eager to do it, but they would be easily handled in the media war that followed.

And he had already ruled out the Billy Jerome approach as being something the handlers would almost certainly reject.

Then, while he was semi-sleeping, something else hit him. Why not the *other* veep candidate? Keith had been telling him some amazing stories about Del Martin's behavior in the campaign offices, and the utter inability of any of the staff to make any sense of it. For Keith, who was evangelical himself, the whole thing was as plain as something that was . . . that was pretty plain. If Del wanted off the ticket, which Keith thought he did, then going out with a bang might be the way to do it. If the initiative for his departure came from within the campaign, they would have to do something damaging to him in order to justify it. But if Del knew that his days were numbered anyhow, it could make sense for him to get out in front of it. At least that is what Keith had told Larry, and Larry was chewing on it now. This could be just the ticket.

Larry had been thinking that the best thing to do, if they couldn't get it done in some place that would create an impossible-to-ignore traction, would be for him to publish the emails himself in the Ecosense newsletter. But he and those three guys in the email thread were mortal enemies already. Half the people that read them would think that Larry was just having a little fun and had just made them all up.

But this idea was a hummer. Del Martin, vice-presidential candidate for the Democrats, *he* could do it. All he would have to do is mention the emails, and a summary of their import, during the vice-presidential debate that was coming up. It would be perfect. Keith had told him that staffers at the campaign were already making worried noises about Del. "He's not the same man he was at the beginning of the campaign," one of them had said.

"That's really true," Kara had said, trying to keep the catty whine out of her voice. As Del's former mistress, she had not taken kindly to her dreams and ambitions being peremptorily side-lined the way they had been. She had cultivated that relationship with Del for *months* before she had tricked him into thinking that he was seducing her. And then to be set aside, somewhat abruptly, had been hard on her views of herself, which—truth be told—were somewhat elevated. Or, if not elevated, at least higher than her current position, and higher, perhaps, than a strict interpretation of the data warranted.

The point of such reports, rumors, grumbles, and complaints, Larry thought, was that Keith had said that it seemed to him that some in the campaign were starting to think about replacing

Martin, and that it also seemed to him that Martin was more than halfway looking for a chance to jump ship. Larry rolled the options around in his mind. So Martin could just stagger on until there was a messy parting of the ways, and judging from what Keith was saying, that could be just a matter of time. Or Martin could just make it to the night of the debate, hoist the Jolly Roger in front of everybody, and have the whole thing done as a clean break inside of two days. And the emails would then be a story that no one could smother with a pillow.

Larry jumped out of bed, almost ran to the shower, and just a few minutes later started to dress hurriedly. He needed to talk with Jill. *This was perfect.* The only way it might not be perfect, he acknowledged to himself, was that not everybody thought about life in the same way he did. Not everybody would think to make a green-friendly statement by having a Hummer running outside their office all the time, say. Maybe Del Martin wouldn't want to immolate himself on national television. That was certainly possible. Not everyone can avoid being a sissy. But . . . perhaps Del would *want* to be dumped from the ticket in a way that didn't involve scandal, or a contrived and alleged scandal, but rather was a situation that was a clear matter of principle, right out there on the surface.

He had to talk to Jill. He was already down in the parking garage. He hopped into his Jeep, chuckling to himself. He thought that Keith would be willing to hand a nondescript thumb drive to Martin. *This is perfect.* It was no doubt contrary to some trifling regulation of the Secret Service, but Keith's job was to protect Del, and this was protecting Del.

It would be about ten minutes to Jill's apartment, and so he called her quickly to see if she was still home. It was Thursday, so he knew she didn't have to go into the senator's office as early as she usually did.

"Hey, Jill. Larry. Can I swing by? I have a really hot idea."

"Sure, I don't have to leave for an hour yet." Besides, she thought to herself, *you can swing by any time you like. Swing on by. I wish you would swing by more frequently than you do.*

"*But!* . . ." she said, before he could hang up, "I am across the park, the one out front of the apartment house. I came over here to get a coffee and bagel, and the line was way longer than anticipated. I was going to grab something, and then go back and grab Piper for a walk. Could you just get her and then meet me at the fountain in the middle? We can give Piper her walk, and you can try to persuade me that you do in fact have a hot idea. I promise to be open-minded."

"How will I get in?"

"Shelly next door is still home. She keeps a key just in case for me. She knows you're a friend, as I had to explain to her several times last week. She couldn't get over how big you are. She thought you had to be at least two friends. She will let you get Piper, and I will text her now just in case."

"Deal. See you at the fountain."

About twenty minutes later, Larry was standing by the elevator doors on Jill's floor, with Jill's spaniel Piper running around his feet in an agitated manner. The doors opened, and two middle-aged women, the previous denizens of the elevator, both gasped inaudibly when Larry stepped through the elevator door. It seemed to them that he filled the door first, and then after that he practically filled the elevator. Once Larry turned around to face the doors, they both moved silently back to the back wall.

Piper, meanwhile, was busy wrapping the leash around Larry's right leg. He looked down, and patiently unwound her. When she looked as though she was going to start right up again, Larry spoke to her sternly. "Sit," he said. A moment later the elevator dinged them as arriving at the lobby, and so Larry turned to let the two women disembark first. His mouth opened suddenly, and then shut again like a trap.

The two women had obeyed his command and were both on the floor, seated with their backs against the wall, legs stretched out, purses beside them. Larry looked at them, aghast, and they stared back at him, terrified out of their minds. Their eyes were bulging.

"Oh, ladies!" He said. He stretched out his hand and they shrank back halfway into the metal wall. There was nothing for him to do but retreat out of the elevator as unobtrusively as he could manage, which was not very.

A few minutes later he and Piper emerged into the sunshine, and Piper repaid him by not running around his leg anymore. She was out in front, straining against the leash. They walked for about five minutes, straight ahead, until they saw Jill waiting for them, seated on the edge of the fountain. *What a fine woman*, Larry thought. *I need to do something about this. Something other than just swinging by. She's not scared of me. Not like those ladies in the elevator.*

Jill had just finished her bagel, and was now working away at her coffee. As Larry and Piper approached, she got up, smiled at him, and reached out her left hand for the leash, thinking that, as Piper was her dog, she should hold the leash. But instead of handing over the leash, Larry shifted the leash into his left hand, and took her outstretched hand into his, and turned left to take a turn around the park.

"Um . . ." Jill said.

"Let me tell you my idea," Larry said. "It's a corker."

"Okay," Jill said.

THAT CODY

One of the things that Rocco had decided to do, almost on a whim, was to place someone every night, after it got dark, just a bit up the street from Helen's condo, and Cody's apartment across from it. There might be something they need to get or pick up, depending on what they are planning, and it wouldn't hurt to watch. Passports maybe?

And that Saturday night, the day after they had met Larry and Jill, this is exactly what Cody and Helen decided to risk. They had made no plans, but they thought they should get their passports, just in case. If they had to do some serious bolting, they really would need the passports, and they couldn't pick those up at a Walgreen's. And while they were back home, for just those few minutes, Helen thought she could pick up a more comfortable pair of shoes, and Cody was going to grab a jacket.

The man that Rocco had put on this detail was a surly one, a rough customer named Woody. He was a bit older, but fully capable of this kind of assignment, and he slouched a bit when a car drove up past him, turned around, drove past him again, and then parked about fifty feet from the two condos, and about fifty feet from where his car was parked. Helen got out and walked up to her place, and when she reached it, she stooped and pulled out an extra key from under a flower pot on the porch. In the meantime Cody had simply walked up to his place, holding his keys in his hand. They both disappeared.

Woody got out and walked down toward their car, and took up a place behind a tree that was just behind the car. He checked his surroundings—the neighborhood was desolate. This was perfect. He pulled his gun out, and just stood there at the ready.

Cody came back out first, and simply stood beside the driver's side, waiting for her. After about three minutes, she came bounding down the stairs. Woody waited until she was about five feet from the car, just when Cody started to open the door. That was the moment he stepped out into the street, gun level, and said, "Hands up, both of you." The gun was pointed straight at Helen, which Cody saw, and slowly raised his hands. Helen did the same.

"Okay," Woody said. "My rig is back this way. Put your hands mostly down, in case somebody is watching." As they were walking toward the car, Woody unlocked it, and then told them to open the back doors, but not to get in. The whole time, he was covering Helen.

He told Cody to stand by his back door, and to put his hands on the roof of the car. Cody did so, muttering to himself about Helen's gun, which was under the front seat of his car.

Woody had Helen sit inside, and he pulled out some zip-ties, and fastened her wrists to the head rest. He closed the door and walked around to Cody. "Same drill," he said, and Cody nodded a little glumly. Woody knew his business, and presented Cody with no opportunity to do what he was yearning to do, which was to take a swing. In a moment, Cody was zip-tied, looking across at Helen. "Sorry," he mouthed to her. She nodded.

Woody got onto his phone as soon as he pulled out, and Rocco answered right away. "We're in luck, boss," Woody said. "Got 'em both."

Cody and Helen could hear some exciting murmuring.

"No, no, I didn't. I knew the other guys had orders, but I didn't. I am taking them to the warehouse. You there? You can think about it, and tell me what to do with 'em when we get there. Happy to do whatever."

Don't like the sound of that, Cody thought. *Who would?* Helen thought.

Woody hung up, and drove in silence. The warehouse, wherever that was, was about twenty minutes away. Cody thought briefly that they weren't blindfolded because Woody was assuming something particular about the nature of the "whatever" that would be assigned to him.

They had been driving in an industrial park sort of area almost the entire time. Not being blindfolded hadn't helped any—Cody didn't recognize where they were at all. They were now driving along a rickety chain link fence, and the car suddenly pulled into a parking lot that wrapped all the way around a huge metal warehouse that had a faded sign on it that said something about furniture on it. Woody drove briskly around to the back, and he pulled up to a spot next to a solitary back door. There was one other car on the other side of the door, and it was a very nice car indeed.

Woody snipped Helen's zip tie first, and brought her around to Cody's side. He then waved her to the side, keeping his gun on her, and then with his left hand snipped Cody's zip tie. Then he backed away, and nodded to both of them to move toward the back door.

They walked into a dim hallway, lit by bare yellow light streaming out of an office halfway down the hall on the right. Cody and Helen made their way to the doorway, where they both hesitated. "In," Woody said.

There was a short couch on the far wall, and Woody brusquely ordered them to it. On the right side was an armchair in which sat one Rocco Williamson, a man who appeared to be about as pleased as a hen with twelve chicks. "Well, well," he said. "Shall we get acquainted, you and I? I feel like I know you two very well already . . . at least I know your circular driving patterns."

He sat drumming his fingers on the arm of the chair. It was a very nice chair, one that matched the couch, and was left over from the furniture warehouse days.

"Are we love birds yet?"

"No," Helen said, but she said this at the same time that Cody said, "Yes."

Rocco laughed. True to form, he was dressed to the nines and, also true to form, he picked a bit of fluff off his right sleeve, and dropped it to the floor. Having satisfied himself that he was presentable, he turned to Helen first. "You are the cause of all this trouble, are you not? The people who were concerned that you might be about to spread . . . um, rumors about them told me all about you. Have you anything to add?"

One of those, Helen thought. A certain kind of movie had killers in them who always wanted to talk beforehand. *Fine with me*, she added to herself. *Stall, stall.*

But all she said was, "Not rumors. Just the truth."

"Perhaps not now, dear. The winners get to define what is and is not a rumor. Only fair."

With that he turned to Cody. "But you, my fine fellow, I know very little about you. You are named Cody, and you are the unfortunate but kind-hearted neighbor who gave this little lady a ride."

"My name is Cody Vance," Cody said.

"And what do you do to keep the wolves at bay? How do you make your living?"

What is this? Cody thought. "Up to just recently, I taught New Testament at Liberty University."

"Ah, a noble vocation, a nob . . . *wait* a minute. Did you say Cody *Vance*?"

"Yes, Cody Vance."

With that, Rocco lurched forward in chair, quivering in excitement. Helen was staring at him in disbelief, occasionally glancing at Cody. *What is this?* she was thinking, right after Cody had thought it a second time.

"Are you the same Cody Vance who wrote *The Handbook on First Century Manuscripts?*"

Cody's eyebrows were about as far up his forehead as they would go. "Yes, yes, I wrote that. That was a reworking of my dissertation . . . at St. Andrews."

Helen was now staring at Cody, not knowing whether to be thrilled or exasperated. *You cannot be serious . . .*

Rocco was sitting back in the chair, holding his stomach, and laughing. He laughed for a full minute, and then chuckled for a few moments after that, as though he was running out.

"Well, I must say, Dr. Vance, it is a *pleasure* to meet you. You would have no way of knowing this, of course, but one of my side hobbies is that of collecting manuscripts. About a week after I obtained and read your delightful little treatise, I had occasion to make a purchase which a week before I would have done without hesitating. But your little book gave me pause. And in the event, that moment of hesitation saved me about $250,000. Greatly in your debt, my boy, *greatly* in your debt."

Cody and Helen both just stared at him.

Rocco sat forward in his chair again. "Seriously. What can I do for you two? *Anything*. Happy to do it."

"Um," Helen said. "Have your, um, assistant drive us back to our car?"

"Done," he said promptly. "And I will settle accounts with old Lee later. He might think I owe him some money. I might not think so. Asking me to put a hit on Cody *Vance?*"

The three of them looked at each other. "If I might be so bold," Cody said, "I think you should retire from the line of work you appear to be in. Help make the world a finer place."

"Well, that's a tall order, sonny. But tell you what. I *will* think about it. Been thinking about it anyways. Opera is no good here anymore anyhow."

They all sat quietly for another moment. Rocco wasn't saying anything, and Cody and Helen couldn't think of anything that they possibly could say.

Rocco looked up suddenly, and called to Woody, who was standing respectfully out in the hallway. "Woody!" He said. "C'mere." Woody appeared in the doorway.

"Woody, take these two back to their car. Treat 'em nice on the way."

CHAPTER 9

Regnant Eco-Nonsense

STIRRING THE POT

In the meanwhile, Steven Lee was not sitting around. He knew that if Helen were not dealt with appropriately, nothing he did would matter. But he also had been around long enough to know that he ought to get some other things set in motion regardless. Or irregardless. He was never sure.

The fact that the emails hadn't appeared yet on some right-wing blog meant that they were almost certainly going to go for the big splash. It occurred to him that her motives might be mercenary, and she might at some point offer to sell the emails back to him, but he somehow doubted that. She had been a true believer in climate change, he was sure of that, the *truest* of believers. If there is one thing that disillusioned true believers are most likely to do, it is go over to the other side. Ex-true believers lurch. They are not on a dimmer switch, especially if you send a couple of buffoons over to their house to kill them. They take that ill. Steven felt confident in his bones that she was looking for a way to put the emails into play politically in a big way. She could probably monetize that anyhow, and really get back at him at the same time. She had never liked him, he was confident of that.

But even if Rocco succeeded in shutting her down—Steven still had enough of a memory of a conscience to avoid words like *kill*—the emails could very well have been reproduced, and still wind up one some right-wing blog. Thus far Steven Lee was tracking in a striking way with how Larry had already advised Helen and Cody. If that happened, Steven wanted the emails to wind up on a really strident right-wing site, because that kind of thing would be the easiest to discount, discredit, or, if it got into Alex Jones territory, simply ignore.

And if that kind of thing were needed, it needed to be in motion already. Steven Lee had a few IOUs that he could call in over on the Hill, and he thought he could get some hearings going on that Larry Locke guy, and his Ecosense. He had actually been planning to do that anyhow, as Locke had become a force to be reckoned with over the last year or so. His first book had sold millions, but the sales were largely limited to the red state choir. That is where his money came from, but what had been worrisome to Lee was the fact that Locke was starting to get some traction as a serious writer, of the kind that scholars did not have to apologize for citing. Lee had noticed a couple instances of *that* just over the last couple of months.

The thing that really rankled was the fact that Locke had published a monograph that had simply dismantled a paper that Lee had presented at Cambridge the previous fall, and which had been subsequently published in *Nature*. Locke's response had gotten some publicity and traction, and the nature of the critique was to look up all of Lee's footnotes in order to show that at least five of the sources he had cited had actually said something quite different than what Lee had told the assembled graybeards at Cambridge. The fact that Lee was no longer an ardent believer in climate change meant that he was no longer nearly as careful as he had been in the early years. His slip was starting to show, which also meant that his slips were starting to show. *Nature* had even been pressured enough to publish some corrections in fine print in the next issue, in the back of the magazine, in eight-point font, but still, it had been embarrassing.

He had only been a true believer for a couple of years at the beginning because he had been intelligent enough to figure out what was going on with the numbers. But by the time he figured it out completely, he was already floating on an inner tube down a lazy river of cash grants, and he realized that if he told the world what he now knew, that lazy river of cash grants would go flow somewhere else.

It was in the following year that he had teamed up with Martin Chao and Leonid Ravinsky, once he had inadvertently discovered their secret atheism—they did not serve the god of climate change, although they were ordained priests in the Temple. Lee had been sharing a beer with them, late one evening after some global crisis conference, and it was getting really late, and Chao had hoisted at least four beers before making a joke about the climate change farce, and the *idiots* who believed in it. Lee had stared at Chao, and Chao had stared back, and Ravinsky had stared at both Chao and Lee, and then Lee glanced over at Ravinsky before bursting into laughter. "You *too*?" he had asked. "Does *anyone* believe it? I mean . . ."

"Oh, almost all of them do," Ravinsky had said. And since that time, the three of them had enjoyed the kind of life that an oriental despot might envy. Peeled grapes, tapestried barges on the Nile, a long line of nubile activists, the lot.

Steven Lee dragged himself back into the present, and shook his head vigorously. The Republicans controlled the House, but the chair of the Subcommittee on the Environment could be rolled kind of easily, or at least had been before, and the IOUs that Steven could call in were from the ranking member, along with three others. If the four of them got the wind in their sails, he thought they could jostle the chairman into agreeing to hearings on Ecosense. After all, Larry Locke had been running that Hummer for months, and it had been kind of provocative—on both sides of the aisle.

Steven Lee scrolled through his contacts, and found the names he wanted. He would spend the next twenty minutes on the phone, and he thought he could guarantee hearings, and then in the morning he could call some reporters up and get a drumbeat going.

BEFORE CONGRESS

Jill stood behind the long wooden table, and looked across the intervening space to the even longer raised and curved bench, where all the congressmen would soon be sitting. About twelve photographers were seated on the floor in between. Their cameras always reminded Jill of short, black bazookas. Or maybe potato guns.

She swallowed, and was surprised at how dry her mouth had suddenly gotten. Jill had been in hundreds of these hearings, and was struck at how different it felt when you were going to testify, as opposed to what she usually did, which was hand Sen. Hart notes that had suggested questions for the witness. Now *she* was the witness. She was the one who was going to be grilled.

This whole thing was a joke. Some kind of rumor must have gotten around the climate change rank-and-file that something bad for their cause was circulating and was loose out there. They were not sure when it was going to drop, but when it did, it would be real trouble for every last pure thought on their agenda, and so, returning to their standard playbook, they decided that the best defense was a good offense. This had resulted in them opening an investigation of Larry Locke's Ecosense, which was actually something they had been wanting to do for a while anyway. It was their understanding that money was absolutely *flowing* down there, and to causes they thoroughly disapproved of. They always disapproved of money flowing anywhere but through them. Money in politics was not necessarily corrupting. However, *other* people's money in other people's causes was most definitely corrupting, and was a corruption not to be tolerated.

Jill turned around, and was grateful to see Larry seated in the back row. He liked sitting in back rows. That way he wouldn't block anyone's view, and he could also be more or less unob-trusive, as much as it was possible for him to be unobtrusive. Larry was scheduled to testify tomorrow. The whole thing had been sloppily arranged by those who had arranged the hearing, but they had still had enough sense to put Larry later, and yes, their enterprise was a total fishing expedition. They had noth-ing, but just wanted to grandstand for the cameras in an effort to dominate the current news cycle, and if it slopped over into the next news cycle, perhaps they would be in a position to shout down whatever it was that was coming. And what was coming? Whatever that nebulous rumor was, it sounded like a bad hit for their movement.

She heard some bustling behind her, and turned to see a row of congressmen coming in, tailed by their aides and other Cap-itol Hill riff raff. She took her place by her chair and prepared to be sworn in.

The lead congressman on the investigation for the Democrats was an odious little man named Harrison Cramond-Ross. His name made it sound like he was a true Ivy Leaguer, and he had a button-down shirt that looked like it, and he was representing a district in Connecticut, which made things even more suspi-cious, but all of that was veneer work—oak veneer on particle board. He had come from a blue-collar family, and had got-ten his education, such as it was, from Ball State, and then he fought his way up through the Teamsters. His little simian nose meant that some of his fights had gotten a little personal, in that his adversaries would taunt him about it. But they were all very sorry now, either that or dead. His name at that time had been a bit more pedestrian—Dwayne Dawkins it had been. He changed his name two years before his first congressional run, which was unsuccessful, and every run since, all six of which had been successful. He was an ugly little man, and dapper, and what he didn't know about dirty politics wasn't worth knowing. He looked like a civilized man, but if you looked straight in his brown eyes, you could see the sewage pumps. On a bad day you could smell them.

"Do you happen to know Larry Locke, the director of Ecosense?" Harrison Cramond-Ross asked Jill.

"Um, yes sir, I do."

"And in what capacity do you know him?"

"Friends."

Jill knew the congressman's ways, and knew that he was going to ask something that was out of line or over the line, and that he would draw a rebuke from the chair. But rebukes from the chair did not have the capacity to unring the bell, and so whatever it was that was said was still going to be out there, poisoning the well. She had resolved that morning in the shower that she would *not* let him do that to her.

"Would you say that you were his girlfriend?"

There was some shouting from the far end of the bench. "Mr. Chairman! This is outrageous! And we are not even five minutes into the hearing! What *is* this?"

Jill signaled to the chair. "I don't mind answering the question."

"Go ahead," he said. He was a kindly one, Rep. Jasper Compton, an elderly gent from Tennessee, and who looked a lot like Col. Sanders, some of which was actually on purpose.

"These things are hard to quantify, and I am not sure what legal definition you are using, sir. We have dated a couple of times, but he hasn't kissed me yet. So maybe you could tell *me* what that is. It could be quite a help to me personally."

The gallery laughed, and Harrison squirmed in his seat. He was not the kind of person who was happy whenever anybody else was happy. The laughter in the room unsettled him, and made him feel things he did not want to feel.

When the laughter finally subsided, Larry was standing up in his back row. "Hasn't kissed her *yet*," he said loudly, and the room erupted in laughter again.

Jill should have blushed, but didn't, and Harrison had no need of blushing, but inexplicably flushed red anyway, which was totally unnecessary. But his color was more a function of not liking it when others were enjoying themselves, and also not liking the sensation that he was no longer in complete control of the questioning.

"Order, order," the chairman said, tapping the gavel lightly. He had enjoyed the joke as much as anyone.

"As you have visited with your, um, friend, has there been any reason for you to think that Ecosense was funneling money to activist groups?"

Jill nodded her head. "Well, we haven't ever talked about it, but I did know that this is something they *do*. I mean, it is in just about all of their brochures. But if you are asking about any of the internal workings of Ecosense, I can save you a great deal of time. I know nothing whatever at all. I am a nullity as far as all of their operations are concerned."

Huh, Larry thought. *She speaks the truth. But this will be true only for a limited time. A time is coming when Mrs. Locke will drop by and all the staffers will scramble, some to get her coffee, others to get her some water, and others to find her a chair. I will insist upon it.*

The rest of the questioning was perfunctory. Harrison Cramond-Ross had wheeled in his huge well-drilling rig, and now, as a result of his morning of industry, he now had himself his first dry hole. The rest of the day was filled up with other lower-level types—one book-keeper, one marketing guy, and two grant-fulfillment executives. All in all, it was a duddy afternoon, made a little festive in the late afternoon when the chair allowed for the video that Trevor had made about that earnest professor of revolution to be premiered. *That* caused something of a sensation, but it also caused the ecochondriacs to drop their guard. They thought that it was the supposed big problem they had been all worried about, and they knew they could brazen that kind of thing out.

The fireworks were reserved for the following day, when Larry took his oath in order to be able to tell them what he thought. The fireworks happened because he took full advantage of the opportunity to tell them what he thought. But in addition to the fireworks, there was one genuine scare, at least as far as Jill was concerned. And as things unfolded, the scare was the first thing on the agenda.

He did the same thing that Jill had done, and stood by his chair until it was time to be sworn in. Jill, unlike Larry, had sought out a place in the front row. She really wanted to watch, and to watch from up close. She knew how smart he was, having read his book. And she was starting to get some inkling of how quick he was from the handful of conversations that she had had with him. But she wanted to watch him closely under some respectable social pressure. She knew he did fine with criminals and thugs.

The only problem was that he didn't appear to be acting like he was under pressure at all. He appeared to leaning forward slightly, like a race horse waiting for the gate to clatter open. She imagined a thought bubble over his head for him. *When is this thing going to start?*

The same bustle that happened the day before happened again, and the file of important people commenced. The people in the gallery began to settle in their seats, after doing their obligatory double take over Larry's bulk. Larry turned around and faced the front of the room, prepared to raise his right hand and take his oath. That happened, and then Larry took his seat.

"Mr. Locke," Harrison Cramond-Ross said with a sneer, "I believe that you wrote an op-ed that appeared in *The Wall Street Journal* last week?"

"Yes, sir. That is correct," Larry said.

"Were you aware that we have discovered three sentences in that piece, in the penultimate paragraph, that were lifted without attribution from a German climatology skeptic, a man named Klaus Weber?"

A congressional aide had helpfully set up a tripod with a blown-up foam core poster, one that had Larry's full column emblazoned on it, and with the three offending sentences highlighted in yellow.

Jill gasped, and then coughed nervously. *Oh no*, she thought. *Oh no. Good things never last. He's still a nice man. The best of men are men at best.* An anvil had mysteriously appeared deep within her abdomen. Her respect for him didn't know what to do, having been shot in one wing, and she felt like she was hurtling toward the ground. And when she heard Larry laugh out loud, she had never been so amazed at anything in her life.

When she looked up, she saw Larry swiveled around in his chair, looking over the crowd. He was looking for someone. That someone, as it turned out, was his publisher, Ken Corcharan, whom Larry had seen about ten minutes earlier. He smiled when he saw Ken already heading down the aisle to his table. He turned back around to Cramond-Ross, and said, politely enough, "Would it be possible for my publisher to be sworn in? His testimony should take five minutes or less."

Cramond-Ross was shaking his head, but the chairman, as I have mentioned, was an affable fellow. "Sure," he said.

After Ken was sworn in, he took the seat next to Larry, and Jill had perked up considerably. She didn't know why, but she felt that the winds had somehow turned back in a favorable direction. Her wing felt fine again.

Ken launched into it, without any introduction. "Fifteen years ago, after the Delmar incident—I am sure you guys remember that one—I resolved to never let any of my writers be caught in that position again. Whenever one of my writers does something for any outlet other than mine, *I* am the one who submits it. That is what I did with Larry's piece last week. And I have a cyber-safe that all such submissions are copied to at the same time the article is sent to the media outlet. This means that I can prove to anyone's satisfaction that the submission did not have those three plagiarized sentences in it."

Harrison Cramond-Ross was caught, but he gamely tried one more twist. "And so how did the sentences get in there?"

"That would be a question for *The Wall Street Journal*. I would suspect a lowly editor trying to curry favor with the lowlifes of Washington. If you would like to pursue this line of questioning, we can always arrange to call whoever it was as a witness, and we will be able to ask them many awkward questions."

"That will not be necessary," Cramond-Ross muttered into a sheaf of papers that he was tapping on the desk in front of him. That observation turned out to be true enough, because Ken was able to turn the attempted plagiarism hit into a full-length article in the monthly newsletter that Aegis put out, and the lowly editor in question was identified in that article, with a photo and everything, and all the awkward questions were asked by his superiors, soon to be his former superiors.

"Will that be all?" Ken asked. Cramond-Ross nodded curtly, and Ken went back to his seat.

By this point Jill had successfully recovered all her aplomb, while Cramond-Ross had recovered almost none of his. But unfortunately for him, he still had a hearing to steer, and so he resorted to what he thought might be a safe question.

"Mr. Locke, could you please summarize for us what you believe the cause of global warming might be?"

"It depends, sir. If you are asking why the globe is warm at all, it is because there is a huge ball of flaming gas in the sky above us . . ."

And Congressman Cramond-Ross coughed, and interrupted him. "Spare us, Mr. Locke. You know every well that this is not the kind of thing I was referring to. What is your understanding of the crisis of climate *change?*"

Larry answered, and his voice was steady and methodical. "There are layers. First, we don't know that any significant climate change is occurring at all. Second, we don't know, if it is in fact occurring, that is a bad thing. It could well be a good thing, or no big deal one way or another. Third, we don't know, if it is occurring and is bad, that man is in any way contributing to it. Fourth, we don't know, whether or not we are contributing to it, and if it is bad, whether we have any capacity to halt it or slow it down. Other than that, I have no views on the subject."

"And you apparently believe, from that answer, that you have the right to donate money to groups that are climate-deniers?"

Larry coughed politely. "I am happy to answer the question, but I have to correct something first. Language is important. I have never in my life given any money to any group that denied there was climate."

"No, I said 'climate-denier.'"

"And I would wonder in return what a *climate* denier could possibly be, other than someone who denies there is such a thing as climate."

"You know what I mean . . ."

"No sir, I do not. I know what you *want* us to start meaning by it, but I do not know what the thought processes in coming up with such a phrase could possibly be. You apparently want us to think that people who differ with you on the science are the equivalent of Holocaust deniers."

Harrison decided to drop it. "Go on," he snarled.

"Yes, we donate money to various groups that are doing the Lord's work in combating all the regnant eco-nonsense, of the kind we see everywhere."

Jill briefly wondered how Larry knew so many odd words that were still short. *Regnant?*

"And so you acknowledge that you are fighting those who want to save the planet?"

"I acknowledge that I am fighting those who like to pretend to themselves that they are saving the planet. But you don't save a planet—that doesn't even need saving in the first place—by convincing hotel chains to try to get out of washing your towels every day. And showing the guests a little cardboard picture of a cute koala, the one that your unwashed towel will somehow mysteriously save."

Harrison, for all his faults, actually believed that climate change was happening, and so he flushed red. "Everyone needs to do their part," he said.

"The way you do?" Larry's eyebrows went up. "Tell me, sir, how many times have you flown on a private jet to Davos, in order to talk with all the swells there about climate change?"

Larry knew you should never ask a question like that unless you already knew the answer yourself. In this case, it was seven.

Harrison sat sullenly, rummaging through his papers like he was looking for a factoid, or a question, or something. Larry's question remained sort of out there, hanging in the air. So Larry resumed.

"The answer to my most reasonable question is seven. You have flown to Davos *seven* times on your lame crusade to save the planet. Perhaps you have heard about the Hummer that I keep constantly running outside our headquarters? If not, you should have heard about it. Do you happen to know how many years I would have to run that thing in order to burn up as much fuel as one of your gallivanting trips does? The answer to *that* question is about thirteen years, give or take. So multiply that by seven, and you have a side-by-side comparison of our respective carbon belching—you, in your attempts to save us from carbon belching, and me in my modest little efforts to make fun of the whole enterprise."

The hearing went downhill from there, and all the different news outlets showed completely different snippets of it. In some cases, it was hard to believe they were covering the same event.

THE TRAP SPRUNG

Billy Jerome was starting to mull over whether or not he actually wanted to be the vice-president. He wavering in his soul, what there was left of it. Deep down, he really did believe the things he would say in his speeches. Put another way, he agreed with himself. He wasn't just saying things to get elected. He wasn't that kind of hypocrite.

He had been a different kind of hypocrite. He didn't actually live up to the standards that he applauded, particularly in his thought life. But it had been many years since he had strayed from his marriage vows, and his wife Ursula had forgiven him—after a brutal six months in counseling—and he had done right by that staffer Sheila and their most inconvenient boy, Thad.

Critics would call it hush money, but Billy always liked to tell himself that he would have been happy to pay that kind of support even if their ongoing silence had not been necessary for his career. And that reassuring thought might even have been true. He was a kindly man, but weak in some unfortunate places, and strong in the wrong ones.

The visit he had received two days before from a couple of key donors—furniture manufacturers from the Midwest—had delivered the shock. But it wasn't entirely a shock because he had been halfway braced for it ever since his political career had begun to take off. The shocking part was that these two reliable Republican donors were accompanied by a third young man who, as soon as the door was closed, did all the talking. His name was Blake and he was actually an operative with the DNC, and was in full possession of the fun facts with regard to Billy's indiscretion from so many years before.

The two furniture manufacturers were there in their capacity of mules. They brought Blake, and Blake brought the blackmail. They were how Blake was going to get a chance to talk to Billy Jerome, and as a couple of good old boy libertarian donors who had just lately arrived in the big leagues, it had been a piece of cake for the opposition research team to find out about a few facts concerning *them* that could easily land them in prison for three to five years. It turns out that there are behaviors that are widely accepted at libertarian conferences that don't really comport with the laws as they are currently structured. This is particularly the case if we are talking about fifteen-year-old girls, which we are.

And so Blake had visited them a few days before, and explained to them how they were going to arrange for a meeting with the vice-presidential candidate, and they were going to promise a sizable enough check as to gain them a meeting with the candidate, and they were going to take him with them, and then he explained that two things were going to happen at the meeting. First, they were going to hand over the six-figure check to Billy Jerome, making him happy, and then they were going to sit silently while Blake explained the position of affairs to Billy, making him sad, and then they were going to go home and forget about the whole thing.

Billy had been reeling since that meeting. Well, to be more accurate, he had reeled for two days, and then spent the three days after that on the teeter-totter. If he did what they said, his own team would simply think that he had had a bad night. Nobody would know. He could simply let a gaffe slip, and everybody would be disappointed. But that would be all. He could do that and clean up the mess afterwards. He could be the best vice-presidential candidate *ever* after that point.

But he had been in politics a long time. He knew that if they had him over a barrel now, they would still have him over a barrel after he took a dive in the debate. What would prevent them from bringing the screws back again? A sense of honor? Billy chuckled in spite of himself.

Then he grew serious again. They could still roll out the existence of his former mistress and his long-lost son two weeks before the election. And he knew, down in his bones he knew, that this is exactly what they would do. In other words, if he caved, he wouldn't be buying silence. He would only be buying a few weeks of silence. That wouldn't benefit him really at all.

And now that it came to the point, the thing that horrified Billy about everything the most was having to face McFetridge, who had been really decent to him. That was the part he dreaded. "Why didn't you tell us?" would be the question of the hour, and to *that* question there could be no satisfactory answer.

So he could take a dive, but he was canny enough to know that this would just postpone the revelation for a month or so. Wouldn't fix anything. He could refuse to take a dive, and then wait in a cold sweat for the moment that they found most convenient to hang him out to dry. What other options were there?

He could go tell McFetridge himself, and submit a letter of resignation. That seemed kind of drastic, even though he knew full well that it wasn't drastic at all. More like fully appropriate. He wasn't emotionally ready for that yet either. And all these options were why he had been wavering in his soul. Very unpleasant it was.

He even tried praying for a little bit, and after about ten minutes of that he called himself pathetic and lame, walked out to the outer office in a glowering mood and told his driver to bring the car around. Then he huffed back into the office and sat in his swivel chair, glaring at the ceiling. After just a few minutes, which seemed to him like half an hour, his phone buzzed. His driver was out front.

Billy walked out the door, his Secret Service men clustered around him, and they headed out. As he was walking out, an idea hit him. Maybe it was the prayer. But maybe not. *Not sure.*

CHAPTER 10

Broken-Glass-Eating Conservatives

CHOOSING THE BATTLEFIELD

When it came to *standard* preparations for the first vice-presidential debate, both Billy and Del were ready. And if all the other stuff hadn't been going on behind the scenes, it might have been the most interesting vice-presidential debate in years. They were both quick on their feet. They both had mastery of the facts, or at least the facts that they were prepared to talk about. But as it was, with all that other stuff going on in the back rooms, what with all the dirty dealing, it was going to be the most interesting vice-presidential debate *ever*.

At the same time, Del felt like he was dealing with a serious handicap, in that most of his standard talking points on the domestic side of things were things he knew he didn't believe anymore. And he had already resolved that he wasn't going to get out there and straight up lie. Legal abortion for two weeks *after* birth? Seriously? But when it came to foreign policy, he was still alright, and thought he could represent himself in a way that would not cause anyone to get their guard up. And two days before, the network had delivered the agreed-upon order of the questioning to the campaigns, and foreign policy was first. That part should be okay.

And he had also decided that he was going to go out in a blaze of glory before they got to the domestic issues. He had the thumb drive in his pocket, where it felt like it weighed five pounds. He was surprised he wasn't leaning over to the left because of it. Del was excited, actually. He was going to do it. His letter of resignation was already written, and scheduled to send five minutes before the scheduled conclusion of the debate. He was going to leave the campaign, and he wouldn't be chased out by some cooked-up scandal. And he would have done the country a service by exposing the corruption of the entire climate change industry. That was all to the good.

The timing seemed good to him. He knew that Kara had it within her to reflect on their time together in such a way as to manufacture sexual harassment and worse out of it. She certainly had been peeved enough. And in the woke climate of the current Democratic Party, any sexual encounter that the woman afterwards regrets would be handled by the party officials as rape. In this Del was prescient, because Kara had been approached by some top advisors and had actually filed her complaint the day before. It was going to be made public two days after the debate because the campaign thought that

Del was a far better debater, even with his recent wobbles, than the walking incoherence that they thought was most likely to replace him. The Vice-Presidential-Candidate-in-Waiting was a lesbian activist named Casey Dupont-Sunder, currently by a major fluke the junior senator from Rhode Island, and a former professor of queer theory. It wouldn't do to let *her* debate Billy Jerome, which would be like throwing a stick of cotton candy at a flamethrower. In fact, the campaign wouldn't want her to do or say anything. She was there simply to shore up the nut roots base of the party, which was larger than it had ever been, and which had been greatly aggrieved by the selection of Del, a straight, white male who was also straight, and male, and white.

But in the meantime, Billy was wrestling with *his* back-room issues. He *thought* he had figured out a long shot solution to his difficulty. He was going to reveal the existence of his long-lost son in the course of the debate. That idea had occurred to him about a week before, right after he had prayed about it. He had run it by his wife Ursula, who was game, as she had known for years that the secret was going to blow up some time. Why not now?

After that, Billy had contacted Sheila. He had needed to spend half an hour or so with her on the phone, explaining that the situation was going to come out regardless, she was going to have television trucks in front of her house regardless, and that he thought that this was the cleanest way through. She eventually agreed, and after that, the only thing that remained was Thad. He needed to talk with Thad, and Billy wasn't at all sure how that would go. Thad could make a lot of trouble, depending on how woke he was, or depending on how angry he was at discovering who his father was.

Billy had broached that topic with Sheila, when he had gotten around to getting Thad's phone number from her. Sheila had actually laughed out loud. "Oh, no," she had said. "You don't need to worry about the *politics* of it at all. He was only taking those woke classes for the sake of reconnaissance. He has been a broken-glass-eating conservative since sometime in high school. So his foray into woke studies went bust. He was discovered and kicked out of that program after about six months. But he still has no idea who his father is. If he ever asked, I would tell him, and I was going to tell him anyway after he graduated. I think it would be good if you told him. But I have no idea how it will go. He might be really angry on a personal level. But on the politics of the thing? No worries there."

And so Billy had called Thad. He apologized for doing this over the phone, but he couldn't figure out any other way to do it, given the circumstances. After they talked, and Billy had said what he needed to say, which he was about to do if Thad let him, he had figured out a way for them to meet.

With that as the opening, Thad had gone out to a deserted waiting room at his fraternity, and had sat down, trying to process why on earth the Republican nominee for vice-president would call him up and start talking cryptic nonsense. But it was certainly Billy Jerome—that gravelly voice was unmistakable.

"Okay," Thad said. "I'm sitting down."

"Well, it's like this," Billy had said. "I am your father."

And at this, Thad had launched. He wasn't sitting down at all anymore. "*What?*"

So Billy then explained, in broad outlines, the circumstances of what had happened, and how he would love to meet Thad, if Thad was willing. "I was always planning on connecting with you at some point, and telling you the complete story. Ursula—my wife—and I both knew it was going to happen sometime, Ursula more than I, but just didn't know when a good time would be. This attempt at blackmail just set the timer for us."

Thad hadn't committed to anything yet. "So if we were to meet, how would we meet? Without telegraphing anything to the world?"

"All you would have to do is go online to the campaign web site, and fill out an application for an internship with the campaign. I will tell our people to look for it, and then tell them I want to interview you personally for that position. Unusual, but not that unusual, and I will say I have heard through back channels some really good things about you, which I have, and it shouldn't draw any unusual attention inside the campaign."

Thad was sitting down again. He breathed in deeply, and said, "I would love to meet with you."

"Okay," his father said. "Fill out the application tonight, and I will ask somebody at the campaign about it tomorrow."

DEBATE FESTIVITIES

"I might get sacked for this," Keith had said. "But I think it might be the noblest thing I will ever get to do."

Three days before the debate, Larry had given Keith a copy of the thumb drive, along with a general explanation of what was on the thumb drive. Keith was going to be on Del's detail later that afternoon, and he pocketed the drive with satisfaction.

And just as it had happened the first time that Keith had talked to Del, the room emptied out for a moment while Del was trying to shovel prep questions back into his satchel. Keith checked in every direction, and walked up to the table where Del was and placed the thumb drive right in front of him. He had memorized what he was going to say, and so he said it straight out. "I don't know if you even want to leave the campaign. But *if* you do, and if you want to depart in a way that will completely dominate the debate between now and the election, this thumb drive is for you."

Del looked at him steadily. "You have successfully captured my interest," he said, grinned, and pocketed the drive.

But he didn't have a moment to read the email thread until late that evening. When he did, he sat back in his chair and stared at the screen for five minutes. Then he read through the whole thing again, his mouth agape. He sat back in his chair again, rummaging around in his mind for something suitable to say. He finally came up with something his grandmother, an old Southern matriarch, used to say when he was a boy. *Land of Goshen.*

The three days to the debate flew by.

The debate stage was enormous and polished like it was supposed to be marble they had somehow obtained from Kubla Khan's tomb, and the two lecterns, as per the detailed negotiations, were precisely fifteen feet apart. Out at the front of the stage was a long curved desk, of the sort where imposing news anchors sit, and behind that desk were three journalists. There was Chris Wallace from Fox, Niki DeMartinpray from MSNBC, and, in the history-making part of the event, the first trans interviewer in a vice-presidential debate *ever*, a gent by the name of Flora. That was all. Flora. Del managed to look at him without wincing, but reminded himself not to try that too many times during the evening. It might wear his resolve down. Flora was a gender dysphoric equivalent of a moonscape. Pretty bleak.

Chris Wallace brought the event to order, right on the dot, and explained the outline of the evening. Each candidate would get a ten-minute opening statement, and then the questioning from the journalists would begin, and all according to the ordered agreement. Del nodded with satisfaction, and noted that Billy looked composed, but a little pale. But then they were into the questions, and he had no time to worry about that. But about twenty minutes in, something happened, and Del felt like someone had tapped him on the shoulder. *Wait a minute.* He looked up and saw that Chris Wallace had had the same reaction. *Wait a minute.* Niki and Flora had not noticed anything, unless you count their respective reflections from the polished desk in front of them. They were both noticing that.

Billy had just said that he had been talking with his son Thad about the problem with the Russian special forces in eastern Turkey just the other day, and that he thought that this was an extremely timely question. Now Billy had two daughters. He was *famous* for having two daughters, especially after they had made that country album that had gone platinum without anybody knowing who they were until after they were famous on their own. *That* had come out at the Grammys, and where the judges were more than a little peeved that Nicole & Angelica, this pert duo of sprightly up-and-comers, were the daughters of a senator. A *conservative* senator. After that rumpus, which lasted for two weeks, everybody in the country knew that Billy Jerome had two daughters, and only two daughters. They knew this about no other senator, but they knew it about Billy Jerome.

And Del was almost certain he had heard the senator just say that he had just been discussing the problem of Russians in Turkey with his son Thad. Chris Wallace was almost certain he had heard the same thing. Del's eyes met Chris's eyes. *Did you hear that?* Billy Jerome picked up on what they were doing and thinking, and so he paused for a moment before getting into the thickets of Middle-East policies. Or perhaps it was the policies of Middle-East thickets. At any rate, he paused. The thickets could wait.

Chris Wallace stepped in, and asked, "Excuse me, senator. But did you just say you were talking with your *son*?"

"Yes. Yes. He is an intern with our campaign."

There were two sound booths up above the auditorium, one on the right for the Republicans and one on the left for the Democrats. In the back of the Republican sound booth, an advisor to McFetridge was stomping back and forth, swearing and frothing a little bit. Curiously enough, there was an advisor to

Brock Tilton doing the same thing in the Democratic booth. They were even using some of the same words.

"What is your son's name?"

"Thad. Thad Halton. But I just mentioned that in passing. Perhaps I should get back to the Middle-East."

All over the country, journalists were firing up their search engines, and this is why a bunch of them missed what happened next. Billy finished his explanation of how the McFetridge administration would handle this new crisis (which somehow looked exactly the same as all the old ones), and landed the explanation nicely. *Well, the horse is out of the barn now.*

And that is when Flora asked Del to speak to the crisis of climate change, and whether a Tilton administration would declare the country to be in a state of emergency because of the clear and present danger presented by the climate change crisis.

Del cleared his throat. Whatever Billy had *thought* he was doing was soon to be pulverized and scattered to the four winds. He thought that he was making headlines, but the headlines he had briefly made were about to be shouldered out of the way by the headlines that Del was about to make.

"Well, as you know, Flora, the Tilton campaign has a full position paper on the subject, and which definitely supports the need to treat the issue of climate change as a true crisis, a true emergency. However—and I am just speaking for myself here—I don't see how it will be possible to leave that paper as it stands over the course of the next several weeks. The entire global consensus on climate change will have to undergo a radical revision. I have just come into information that reveals that senior figures, key figures, in the climate change world have been running the largest scam in the history of mankind. And I have the proof of this right here."

And Del held up the thumb drive.

MUSHROOM CLOUD

Del's resignation from the campaign as the vice-presidential candidate had been accepted immediately. Nobody even had to think about it. But even though that was sewed up promptly, Del still had had a tumultuous week post-debate. The circumstances of his resignation had prompted demands from the party chiefs back in Virginia that he resign his office as senator. This was something that Del was entirely disinclined to do, not seeing the need, and also because the climate change emails had made life very festive for the state party.

A number of those guys were worried about their own offices, their own positions, not to mention their very own sinecures and fiefdoms. All Del had needed to do to get them all to calm down was to mention the possibility of him switching parties. Apart from the practical usefulness of such a move as a threat to keep those particular hounds at bay, it was a move that was starting to make more and more sense to Del every day that passed. He had even printed out a copy of the Republican Party platform to read over.

The scandal assumed the proportions it did because of all the guffaws and snorts in the emails. The revelation that the lead honchos of the climate change fraud knew that it was in fact a fraud, and had been *chortling* about it to one another in quite an unbridled fashion, is the element that caused the whole scandal to take on the demeanor and outlook of a mushroom cloud.

It would have been bad enough if the emails had revealed that the chief instigators of the climate change racket had *known* that the science was bad, but they were somehow really sorry that the science was bad. If only there had been more brow-furrowing or soul-searching or angst-riddenness or something. But there was *nothing* of the kind. There was no attitude visible in the email thread other than sheer, unrestrained glee. They were writing to one another like three pirates in a Caribbean cave somewhere who, having downed a couple of quarts of rum, had started to throw gold doubloons at one another in that playful way that pirates sometimes have.

They were not wrestling with the ethical issues at all and, following some well-known advice once given by Friedrich Nietzsche, had decided to move beyond good and evil, and to have as good a time as they possibly could while there. Like Vegas, the brochures promised that what happened there would stay there, which turned out, after all the pieces fell out of the sky, not to have been the case.

And this is why it chafed the American public in such a spectacular way. They were already in a state of high annoyance on the issue, having been able to observe climate change advocates fly off to Davos in their private jets, while they were being encouraged to do their part in saving the planet through buying toilets that didn't flush, and shower heads that didn't let any water through, and allowing nosy city officials to monitor the contents of their garbage. But despite all of that, they had managed to keep their annoyance in abeyance by telling themselves that a lot of these people were Hollywood types and couldn't help themselves. They were just trained to recite their lines anyway. They were *actors*, for crying out loud. But when it came out that the ones imposing all the sacrificial burdens on the whole stinking country were themselves yukking it up over the high gullibility of a continent full of chumps, the chumps took it amiss.

These men, and by these men, we refer to Steven Lee, Martin Chao, and Leonid Ravinsky, had fallen prey to the ancient and deep trap that has snared so many who have somehow managed to make it to the top of the world, and by which we are writing metaphorically, and not about the North Pole. Up there on the top of the world, there is a deep pit that is lined with sharpened bamboo sticks, and all covered over with leafy fronds. Out in the middle of those fronds is a bowl of warm bread pudding, pudding that has been cooked in butter, conceit, flattery, hubris, and then covered over with some clotted cream. It is a rudimentary trap, and it is consistently surprising that it continues to work as well as it does. But there it is.

When Del had first read the emails, he knew that he could put them in play as a real political issue, and in a way that the major media would not be able to spike. And he knew that it would be a live issue straight through to the election. But in this he had seriously underestimated how big it would go over. The reaction was far, *far* beyond his expectations.

The country had gone up in a sheet of flame. To be strictly accurate, there were a handful of Maoists in a few English departments here and there who did not contribute to the heat, but everyone to the right of Brock Tilton was outraged, or had to pretend to be.

And this is why Del's resignation from the campaign had gone as smoothly as it had. Among the close circle of Tilton's advisors, the general sentiment was that they wanted to disembowel Del and march around the campaign headquarters with his intestines on a stick. They thought that this would serve as a caution to others. That was what they said behind closed doors while they were venting. But they were also hardcore politicos, and they knew that in that debate Martin had become an American hero. They knew that out in public, it at least needed to *look* like it was something of an amicable parting. And so it was.

At the same time, the crazed base of the party were demanding Del's blood. It was for this reason that they got everything they were demanding when it came to the replacement veep pick. They demanded, and got, someone who, when it came to economics, believed in almost nothing other than her own pure thoughts. They wanted, and they got, a commie. And then, almost as soon as Brock Tilton ended the call in which he extended the offer to Casey Dupont-Sunder, which she accepted, he went into the kitchen to get himself a glass of milk, poured it, sat down at the table there, put his head on the table, and died of a heart attack.

The two major parties were in a state of absolute churn. Del, the number two man, had stepped off the ticket. A nobody lady with glassy eyes and with a yen for totalitarian solutions had replaced him. Then the number one man died on the party handlers, and they were all left staring at one another. Do we promote Dupont-Sunder to the lead slot?

Meanwhile, over on the Republican side, Billy Jerome was in the process of insisting that he step down as well. He was in the middle of the conversation he had so much dreaded, the one with Bryan McFetridge. McFetridge had been gracious enough on a personal level, and extended his forgiveness when Billy sought it. "But," McFetridge had added, "this doesn't let us off the hook. We still have to decide what to do."

Most of his top advisors were in favor of sticking it out, including the one who had been swearing like a pirate in the sound booth at the debate. "No blood, no foul," he said. "When those words first came out of Billy's mouth, I thought we were going to talking about Thad from now to November and, thanks to Del, we won't be." A number of the others nodded agreement. "Leave well enough alone," one of them said. Another one added, "If we pick a new guy, he will just be fresh meat. They will know within two weeks if he ever pushed anybody on the playground when he was in kindergarten. High risk, and no upside. And we have done three internal polls on Billy here, and a *lot* of the women think it is really sweet that he is reunited with his son."

McFetridge looked at Billy. "And yet," he said, "you want to step down."

"Yes, I do," Billy said.

"And how come?"

"Three reasons. First, I think it is the right thing for me to do. I thought about telling your vetting team about it, and I was too scared. I should just own it. Second, this whole thing has drained my ambition clean dry. My Senate seat is safe, and I am ten years older than you, which means that since you are likely to be president for eight years—now that the Dems look to be nominating someone from the Red Guard—it just doesn't make much sense any more. And third, I do agree with what your worthy advisors have just said, and I have an idea for a replacement that I believe will cover all the bases."

"Who?" Five voices spoke at once.

"Del Martin."

Del had left his phone on the coffee table in the living room, and while he and Gina were in a full clinch in the kitchen, it started to ring. "Let me get it for you," Gina said. "I'm closer."

She picked up a few seconds later. "Hello, this is Gina . . . no, no, this is Del's phone. I just picked it up for him . . ."

She walked into the kitchen with the phone, handed it to Del, and said, "You'll never guess."

Ends and Odds

Steven Lee was now safely under arrest, and the federal prosecutor had just decided that it might be easier to go through all the statutes and toss out the ones that *wouldn't* involve a legitimate charge. Martin Chao was at his cousin's house in Indonesia, and was going to be pretty hard to find, and Leonid Ravinsky was at *his* cousin's house in Crimea, and he would be a little bit harder. It would take a while to track them down, and then it would take an even longer while to figure out how to extradite them. And their argument would be that they should not be extradited over a mere disagreement about the weather.

Larry and Jill had a short engagement, and a small family wedding on the eastern shore of Maryland, where the families from both sides met for the first time, and got along famously. They were still getting along famously, and did so for several days, after the couple flew off to their honeymoon. That honeymoon was located on the dream parcel that Larry had bought near Kalispell. "I have to teach her how to chop wood," Larry had joked to the minister at the reception. Jill laughed and flirty-flared at him, saying, "Yeah, well, I have a few things to teach *you* as well."

"Well, okay, then," Larry said.

It took Cody and Helen a bit longer to get to that place of marital happiness, although they did come to Larry and Jill's wedding as a couple. They had to navigate the whole thing very carefully—dating without dating. Cody was calling it evangelism, after which it morphed into something like apologetics and worldview training. The whole time Helen thought he was trying to bring her to the point where she would agree to be baptized, but then discovered, after she finally got to *that* place, that Cody was a Presbyterian who had been teaching at a Baptist university, and that he didn't think she needed to be baptized again at all. She had been baptized when she was twelve, and her whole family was still baptist. She was worried about how *that* was going to go over, but she needn't have worried about it. Her family was a pretty balanced group, and were more than willing to trade an atheist for a Presbyterian. It was like losing a pawn to take a queen.

So that chewed up a couple of months. Even though she had been an atheist for many years, she had been a baptist atheist, and the idea of her atheistic interlude not affecting her baptism took some getting used to. But she really wanted to be on the same page with Cody, and so they had a pretty intense series of Bible studies. After she made her peace with that, and had finally repented of her whole framework of thought, she surprised Cody one Sunday by taking communion with him. She had been attending church with him for some months, but this time when the bread went by, she took a piece. Cody stared at her momentarily, but then reeled it in and got his mind back on the hymn they were singing.

But that was all he had been waiting for, really, and he had the ring hidden in glove compartment of his car. He decided on the spot to take her someplace nice for lunch and propose there, which he did. Helen laughed out loud, and said *of course*, stood up to come around the table to give Cody a hug, and then the wait staff figured out what had just happened, and they gathered around to applaud.

The warning shot to Cody's rear windshield was a puzzler and mystery for about six months. It turns out that the warning shot had come from Sommerville's brother-in-law, an old school redneck from the hinterlands of Virginia. At a family gathering that afternoon, he had heard his learned kin breathing out fulminations over Cody's refusal to pull the article earlier that afternoon, and because he had four beers in him already, it was a small matter to add two more beers, and head on down the road to the Windshield Doctor to see if he might tail Cody from there. The whole thing came out at another family gathering six months later, when numerous beers were again involved, at which time Sommerville called the cops, and wrote Cody the handsomest apology that Cody had ever received.

Without saying anything one way or the other about the presidential election, Del Martin and Gina were very happy together. Gina was converted about six months after Del had been, and it was almost entirely on the basis of how different and entirely changed he was. The fact that he had surrendered his presidential ambitions was the central thing that Gina just couldn't get her mind around. The old Del would not have done that kind of thing, not in a million years But Del had actually done that, had gone and put that on the altar, and had actually seemed eager to do so. And then he had just been given a veep slot again.

His past infidelities had really hurt her, deeply, but she was also astonished at how rapidly his transformation had put all of that into the shade. After a few years under new management, their own earlier marriage seemed to her like a crummy movie they had seen once.

Billy Jerome served one more full term as senator, in which time he spent a lot of time establishing connections for his son Thad. They had hit off like a . . . well, like a long-lost father and son. The man who succeeded Billy Jerome in the Senate made a frightful hash of it, and after six years of senatorial malfeasance, misfeasance, and unfeasance, Thad challenged him in the primary, and won handily.

Trevor and Eve Smith moved out west somewhere and, contrary to her expectations, they continued to hunt together. One year Eve even got a buck before Trevor did.

Montenegro Cash was arrested about two years after all these events on a charge of securities fraud, and was sentenced to ten years.